CROSSROADS IN CASA CORTE

CROSSROADS IN CASA CORTE

ANNE SCHROEDER

WOLFPACK
PUBLISHING
— EST 2013 —

Crossroads in Casa Corte
Paperback Edition
Copyright © 2024 Anne Schroeder

Wolfpack Publishing
701 S. Howard Ave. 106-324
Tampa, Florida 33609

wolfpackpublishing.com

Paperback ISBN 978-1-63977-160-8
eBook ISBN 978-1-63977-159-2
LCCN 2024933660

CROSSROADS IN CASA CORTE

CHAPTER ONE

Corte: (Spanish) A masculine word with many meanings. Like a man's actions. To some, it means to cut, as in the draw of the cards, or with a knife. Justice is swift in Casa Corte.

The outhouse door stands ajar. From a distance, it seems someone has forgotten to close it against the flies. The stench hits him first, the smell of death amplified by the drone of flies. Inside, against the gloom, a slash of yellow—a silk scarf tied around the diablo's neck, stiff with the finality of death. Esquivel swings the door open. Mendoza's knife lies nearby, the gore of his innards cloyed on the blade. The throat slashed. The chest may bear another stab wound, he does not move the torn shirt to see. The man is dead. He stares at the body, but he can summon no more regret than if one of the dogs from the arroyo were lying at his feet.

He glances away and his fingers twitch. What was it Mendoza said—his wish to see the dawn? Another image intrudes, Mendoza, emptying his bowels into the Chihuahua sand without realizing the desert was ready to swallow him as well.

Against the outhouse, flies cluster on the drying blood.

La policía must be summoned. Behind him, his wife is already making the phone call, her face set in hard lines. Too late. On second thought, if it were up to him, he would hold off. Nothing to be gained by bringing trouble into his cantina—how often has Juanita told him the same?

In minutes, the thin ribbon of the roadway yields an approaching vehicle. At the river, the driver downshifts. His tires spin and slide. He grips his wheel and rides out the arc, snaps straight, and continues. It is Fuentes driving. Bad news. Fuentes is a dog of a policeman who does not give up until he finds his prey.

Across the river, the bridge is washed away, torn loose by the flash flood that engulfed the canyon during the night. The river's level has fallen, but the water has torn the bridge from its moorings. Travelers from the desert must ford in the sand, and if the driver is unfamiliar with the conditions, then there is also the quicksand.

Esquivel watches, half-wishing the car would mire and stall or, better yet, turn around and wait for a better day, if one was to be had. Already, there is nothing good to come of this day. One of the men inside has done this deed. He returns his gaze to the automobile. The village is still asleep, the sun a faint glow in the east, but Fuentes is determined. In the river, his tires spew sand until the car jolts forward. Esquivel checks his watch. Twenty-two hours have passed since he slept. When this is settled, he will welcome a bath.

With nothing better to do, his thoughts return to the previous morning, another lifetime, it seems.

CHAPTER TWO

Cortar: To sour, to curdle

The light is anxious this morning, like a virgin before her first kiss. Esquivel Martinez feels its hesitancy as he waits in the yard, his flesh sleep-warm from his bed. In the dawn, he studies the desert's lines through the dark haze, like a lover gazing at his slumbering woman, his eyes straining to see what his mind remembers.

From a nearby yard, he hears his neighbor, the sound amplified against the scrap tin of the haphazard fence that separates them. Tacked together with materials bartered off his customers' trucks, the fence confines him. He feels no greater freedom than the pigs sleeping in the corner under the broken sheet of plywood.

In the pink dawn of the Chihuahua morning, a vagrant breeze ruffles the thatch of silver hair on Esquivel's naked chest. With the faint promise of the coming heat, the breeze stalls and falls away in the desert silence.

His neighbor calls out jokingly because, for him, life is good today. "Hey, amigo! My wife see you out here, she'll be ruined for me."

"*Vale la peña*." Worth the price. Esquivel's cigarette blows smoke back into his eyes and he curses.

"What's wrong, amigo? Not enough sugar in your panoche this morning?

"My wife, she don't make hers with sugar no more!" Esquivel returns the banter to lighten his shame.

"Too bad. *That* sugar's sweet!"

Esquivel shakes off the words, his throat tight with annoyance. "Don't you got somewhere you got to be?" His neighbor's humor dogs his heels as he heads back to his house.

At the door, his neighbor hesitates. "You some sorry dog today, amigo. What direction freedom hiding for you today, my friend?"

"Not north. I been there." Esquivel flicks his cigarette onto the sand and watches it burn out. "The north, she is a great spoiled woman, belching from excess while she tosses us the bones of her meal." He picks a tobacco scab from his lip. "I got nowhere to go. For me, there is only this place."

"Sure. I hear you." His neighbor's laughter disappears into his house.

Alone, Esquivel turns to scrutinize his village, whose shading has grown deeper than it was in the dark of the moon. Like a woman, the light makes it harder to penetrate her shadows. Hunger for a cigarette drives him, but he tries to satisfy his urges with the land. To the east, stunted, flat-paddled *nopal* and round barrel cacti dot the sand, their primeval leaves curled to spines. A seam of salmon, shot through with blood, silhouettes the horizon.

He picks at a scab on his lip and scowls.

The heat will hold off another month until the rains

have ended. Today, the sun brings the bright crispness of a Mexican spring. Through the soles of his feet, the earth feeds the heat. In the summer, the plant life is greedy, unwilling to share the little rain that falls with the *gila*, the horned toad, or the rattlesnake resting beneath a rock. A wise man knows the desert is not a lover, but a woman grown hard from neglect. In the punishing heat of summer, she fights like the dogs.

"*Madre de Dios.* I am an old man. My bones are drying up. One day, their dust will blow to the mountains and disappear." He presses his naked buttocks against the smooth grain of the door and flexes. "My flesh grows soft…like a woman's. I am an old man." His words pierce with the sharpness of a cactus spine, and he winces. If he is not careful, the day will lose its flavor before it has begun.

In the quietness of his yard, he strides barefoot across the packed sand to retrieve a cigarette from a pack he keeps in the crotch of a pepper tree. He lights it, draws deep, and savors the green, unbroken spirit of the day. The cool fingers of morning flutter about him. He looks around, hoping to find something to give him heart, but there are only his neighbors' houses, a few dusty shacks worn smooth by the grit of sandpaper wind, cast for the moment in the gentle colors of the amber sky.

Along the highway to the north, a white cement cross catches the sunrise. Propped up by a pile of smooth stones, it marks the spot where a family has failed. Plastic flowers circle the base of the cross. Already faded, they will outlast the bones of the children who died there. For a moment, he wonders how it would feel to have someone grieve him when he is gone. But he has no son to carry forward his name and no daughters to give him grandchildren.

His eyes wander from the cross toward the narrow

strip of land beyond his fence, an alley through which his neighbors will soon pass on their way to the mines.

Casa Corte is a poor man's village he tells visitors who stop at his cantina. He does not say it by way of apology. There is much that the village lacks, but this lack will provide the children with a goal, and someday the town will be beautiful. Even so, Casa Corte has much to brag about in the deep well from which the women draw their water. Esquivel tells visitors that when Pancho Villa led his army through on a raid to the border, the general's men stopped to water their horses and to refill his touring automobile's steaming radiator before they crossed the desert.

From the corner of his eye, a white dog pisses on a post and continues down the street.

With nothing else to occupy him, he shifts his attention to the urgent squawks of the roosters claiming the mean streets of dawn. The village is laid out in four straight rows on the flat sand, one row hiding behind the other on each side of the highway. The houses are simple, built of creamy concrete blocks that temper the heat. In his desert, land is plentiful—more so than the materials for building. It is the wood that is scarce, and what exists must be reserved for lintels, doors, and rafters where mud and concrete won't do.

The shops stand next to each other. Some have brightly painted overhangs of yellow, blue, and green, marked with the name of the shop painted in block letters. Over the smaller stalls, faded canvas awnings absorb the brunt of the sun and the wind. The sidewalks are a mismatch of textures and heights, poured with whatever each landlord could afford to the edge of his property, some stippled with stones to lessen the cost of the concrete.

At the corner, a faded metal sign advertises *Kodak Film*

sold here. Most of the signs are in Spanish, but their meaning is obvious from the shawls and pots hanging from hooks and the wafting smells. The sidewalks are lined with barefooted Tarahumara Indians who squat on their heels, their wares lain out on blankets before them. Beggars spend their days alongside old blind women, young mothers, and with the boy with the leg deformed from the mercury that still leaches from the mine tailings.

The small mission church in Casa Corte is square and squat, bounding the west side of the Plaza Corte across from the well. Esquivel does not mind that his wife joins the women before each feast day to dust the plastic flowers at the feet of the Virgin of Guadalupe. On feast days, they rub the windows with crumpled newsprint until the glass sparkles.

This week, the town celebrates the fiesta of *El Dia de los Muertos.* The churchyard is filled with tables where children sell holy relics and homemade candy skulls. Esquivel Martinez has no faith in God, but still, he is a Catholic. If there is a God, he thinks, this God must live inside the church because he has searched in the hills and the desert and has not found Him anywhere else. In the hills and the desert, he finds only ghosts.

A car backfires, the sound like a rifle shot in the stillness. Further down the alley, a single light spills through a dusty window. Best he goes inside and clothe himself. His wife will be up soon, and she will complain in her shrill voice if she finds him outside without his trousers.

Fumbling for another cigarette, he listens for her waking noises, but the only sound is the scratch and flare of his match. Sucking deep, nicotine feeds his blood, and his mood grows lighter.

From the arroyo, a pack of dogs tracks an animal left behind, one from his neighbors' flocks. Too bad. Dogs have a mean life. They do what they must to survive.

Like everyone else in the village, they have to fight for the common things. Esquivel listens with a hunter's ear as the pack closes in with frantic yips and howls. When it comes—the sudden and profound silence that measures the kill—Esquivel shrugs. It is a hard way for an animal to die. *Might be that scrawny lamb of Xavier's. Too small to live, anyway. Bad business. The loss will be felt.* "Might be a goat," he mutters. "Damn dogs. Not enough for people to eat, but the dogs always get a bellyful."

A door opens, and his neighbor's angry voice climbs the thin wire fence that chews into the bark of the stunted pepper trees along the fence line. "Hey, Martinez...hear that? Mendoza's dogs again. Killers. Should be *him* someone shoots, not his dogs. Tonight we go hunting, hey amigo?"

"*Tal véz.* Maybe sometime we take care of the problem, amigo." *Night hunting.* In the old days, stalking a jaguar was better than sex. Stalking Mendoza's dogs will be bad business...but it is what must be done. *Ojalá, God willing,* Esquivel thinks.

The neighbor disappears inside again. The air settles, and Esquivel feels his restlessness return now that the sun has topped the arroyo and the dawn belongs to the past. He returns to the house. Inside, he pulls on his khaki trousers while his wife faces the far wall, pretending to sleep.

———

By NINE O'CLOCK, the coolness fades from the cantina. Soon, the village will turn its welcoming face to the highway that brings the tourists from Ciudad Juárez. In another hour, he will hear them haggling with vendors beneath the narrow awnings. They haggle because they have been told it's expected, and some of them do it poorly. When they have filled their bags and satchels, the tourists will focus their cameras on the melancholy women who track the sun's path with their faded eyes from the shadows of the milk-colored buildings.

At eleven, Esquivel will open his doors beneath the hand-painted sign that announces his cantina. Tourists will stop to buy a drink or to eat a meal of tortillas and frijoles with *mole*. His cantina is an exception to the drinking houses he has visited in Mexico. The only such establishment in his small village, *Esquivel's* welcomes anyone who desires a drink—or who has need of a meal. No mean bar on the backstreets where knives and blood claim the lives of the men who tempt their fates with others of their kind. Neither is his cantina a cocktail lounge like in the resorts where *turistas* in polyester blue leisure suits drink margaritas and scotch.

Esquivel's opens its doors and the village comes. Each day brings surprise. The north may claim to know democracy, but Esquivel serves freedom with every bottle. His wife serves *frijoles* and *mole* so that when her time comes, she will not have to stand before her God and confess that she did less than she could.

The tough men and the fighters take their business north—into Cuidad Juárez—where the spoils are more to their liking. It is mutually agreed that the men who drink at *Esquivel's* leave their knives in their belts for the coyote pelts and the castrating of calves. After the headache of drinking passes. A fact that Esquivel backs up with the help of *la policia*, who patrol the isolated stretch of road that connects Casa Corte with the highway.

A poet from San Antonio who once waited out a radiator repair at one of his tables tacked a page on the wall:

Esquivel's is like an old woman with warm tortillas to

offer. Her worn hands put them forth in such a way that
her friends know she is happy to share.

Esquivel leaves the writing alone, but he does not like to think that his wife is old.

The years have wrought changes in Maria Juanita Martinez. She has grown silent, her sparkle steadied to a cautious and muted regard. Her waist has thickened, and her hips seem wider now. She lacks the cheekbones of beauty. And the stature. But the desert sun does not yet line her face; her skin is smooth and supple.

In the mornings, she sweeps the dirt at the entrance to the cantina without singing, wipes dust from the plain wooden doors and featureless windows without seeing the small raw block building. The entry alone interests her, a heavy wooden door that stands out in the brilliant blue of the Virgin of Guadalupe's robes, painted by her own hands when she was a young bride so everyone would know that hers was the abode of a righteous woman and a Catholic. Above the arch she added six gold stars that have kept their color even as the door has faded. Although it can no longer compete with the shouting lavender of the Jehovah's Witness Hall at the edge of town, it is of no matter. The color satisfies her.

In the early days of her marriage, at fifteen, the town watched her sweep her husband's yard with a new broom he brought from Chihuahua, its straw tied with an electric stitching machine to a green handle that fit her small hand. She swept the concrete floor of her small house in the way she learned from her mother. The desert was generous. More sand greeted her each morning until she wore that first broom to a stub, and many more after that. But she found an old Indian man in her village who tied his own brooms and sold them to feed his family, so she bore down harder than she might have, had the new brooms come from Chihuahua, like the first.

In the coolness of the morning, Juanita draws her dusting cloth across the door and latches it against the sunlight while her lips move in prayer. "Holy Mary, Mother of God, pray for us sinners now and at the hour of our death…"

CHAPTER THREE

E squivel keeps to himself, shining a glass with a worn bar towel, his mind wandering. His thoughts are the only things his wife does not possess, and he needs them for himself. His wife is like the rest of his neighbors. They had no choice, but for him, living on the desert was an accident. The difference sets him apart.

In the morning, he reads his mail from Chihuahua, and sometimes the *Mexico City News*, a day late. Early afternoons, when business is slow, he reads behind the bar: philosophy, Hemingway and other American writers he discovered in school, Gabriel Garcia Márquez and Carlos Fuentes from books he borrows from the library at Chihuahua. He likes the heat of knowledge in his head. Sometimes he reads in English, sometimes in Spanish, both languages living connections to his past.

Esquivel is not Mexican. Some of his customers have

forgotten, or they have forgiven him the accident of his birth, but he carries his boyhood buried in his head, a story he shares with no one, a time when he was a boy named Ernie, living in San Francisco. He never knew his father, only that his mother carried a sailor's passion long enough to make a baby, then used her wiles on a succession of boyfriends while she supplemented welfare checks with her street art to feed them.

The grandmother he remembers was half-French. He once spent a summer at her house in Coronado. When he was ten, he tried to learn French from a tape recorder, but the work was hard. With no one to practice on, the lessons didn't take. Six years later, Mexican became the language of his survival. He learned it from the streets, the curse words and idioms—the words for fornication, food, and making money.

The past sours in his head this morning. What is it about this day that leaves his nerves on edge, as though the desert winds are waiting to cover his cantina with their fury? But the air is calm. There is nothing to set this day off from the one before. Only the feeling that he is waiting.

Outside, the mountains catch the rain that should rightfully belong to the village and the farmers. Somewhere in the highlands, a storm is brewing. Maybe tonight the mountains will unleash their fury on all that waits—people, dogs, the land. If so, it will be a slow night; the regulars will stay in their houses, afraid to cross to the other side of the arroyo, even for a drink. Only the unwary, or the stupid—or the indifferent—will bother.

His eye catches a glossy sheet of paper newly taped to the wall, a photograph of the beach at Acapulco clipped from a magazine. His wife's doing. She does not know about the girl, or she would not be so cruel.

"Madre de Dios!" The taste of bile sours his tongue. He swipes the paper and crumples it into a ball, lobbing it at the fireplace while his wife cringes in surprise. *"Madre!"* He wraps his towel around a whiskey glass and scowls, but she knows him too well to be afraid, so the bluff is wasted.

Reluctantly, he recounts his memories of Acapulco. Sometimes the story gets mixed up in his head. He confuses the things he did and said with the things he wishes he had. Today, his mind is clear. It was 1966, back when he was still a *gringo*, heart and body, forced to ride into Baja to pick up a shipment that would pay his mother's bills. But the plan did not go as expected. At the end of the day he would find himself alone in Oaxaca, a refugee, an orphan, a *Mexicano*. By then, his mother would be on her way back to San Francisco in her asshole boyfriend's van, driving through the jungle without him. And he would be on his way to the fishing village.

Today, in the cantina, the boyfriend's name is almost as faded as the memory of his mother's face.

———

RAY! The boyfriend's name was Ray. In his head the sun beats down on the battered 1961 Volkswagen van, its clutch hot from the way Ray jammed the gears through the rutted, twisting road to the pick-up spot. For two hours, the four *banditos* in drab jungle uniforms shouted insults and threats and brandished their rusty carbines. When they tired of their game, collected their money and faded into the jungle, Ray took out his humiliation on the kid who had witnessed his cowardness.

Crouched in the muddy track, Ernie half-hoped the men would return. He was only seventeen, but he knew that if they decided to backtrack, to take the drugs as well as the money, they would leave no witnesses. That thought kept his hatred from exploding inside him like a ripe tomato.

"Load up, dammit! Load!" Ray's command was only a pretense. They both knew it didn't matter. The kid's timing would be an excuse for Ray's fist.

Ernie planted his feet and braced for what he knew was coming. Ray's first blow knocked him to his knees, but hatred blunted the pain. "Come on, you bastard! Is that all you got?" When the next blow broke his eardrum, he wiped the fluid off his cheek with the back of his hand. "I hurt feelings harder than that, you son of a bitch!"

"Ernie, don't—" His mother's voice sounded like a squawking bird until a balled-up fist across her mouth silenced her scream. Blood dripped from her pressed fingers while she shook her head, a warning for her son not to make trouble, but Ray hit her again, this time splitting her lip with his gold knuckle ring.

At that moment, Ernie felt the tomato burst. Blood-red fury filled his vision as he seized a tire iron from where it lay next to the spare tire and gave Ray a final lesson about pain.

When he and his mother finished packing kilo bricks in the spaces between the lining and the metal of the van's panels, he stuffed one inside his sleeping bag. A gift from Ray. Later, he would sell it off in pieces to college boys on the beach to pay for his lobster traps. He had planned to stick another brick beneath the driver's seat in hopes that the border guards would find it, but no need to now. Ray wasn't returning to the States.

"Go, Mom. Don't stop for anything." Then he ran.

When he mumbled his name, *Ernie di Salvo*, to the first Mexican he met, the words competed with the squawking of a brilliant yellow parrot hiding in the forest canopy. The Mexican man repeated what he heard, "Esquivel. So you need a ride, eh?" And the name stuck.

That was 1966, a long time ago. He never learned if his mother made it back across the border.

On the beach, the seabirds woke him each dawn in time to stow his sleeping bag in a friend's shack before the flat-bottomed fishing boat left the bay. In the inky darkness, he helped Jose drag the boat from the edge of the jungle down to the water. At first, he was just another hand to pull in the nets, but he learned quickly. Within a week, his fillet knife could pass through the gills and open the belly of a red snapper as quickly as Jose's.

"Hey, Jose—I got your back, comprende?"

He slept beneath the banyan trees that first summer, with a machete beneath his sleeping bag for marauders and a piece of stout bamboo for the Brahma cows that wandered past on their way to the water's edge.

The locals allowed him to join their basketball team because he was tall and quick. At nine each evening, when the heat died down, the local boys made room for one another around the edge of the dirt court and cheered him between mouthfuls of burritos bought from vendors in the plaza. Soon everyone knew the name of the tall *gringo* who swished baskets over the heads of the smaller boys. They shared their mezcal with him, and their card games, and Esquivel learned the idioms of their language while the summer passed in a blur of humidity and the faint smell of fish.

The girl appeared one morning. Esquivel watched her swim while sunrise exploded over the mountain in a halo of light. By the time she returned to the shore, the fishing boat had left without him.

He rose the next morning and waited beside the bay, shadowed by a clump of pampas as she swam naked. When she stood and walked from the water's edge, beads of moisture glittered like rhinestones on her golden skin. He forgot to breathe. She turned when she saw him and smiled slowly before covering herself.

"Are you a silkie?" he asked. Her skin had the sleekness of a seal, smooth and scented with olive oil that she rubbed onto her body after her swim.

"I am from Greece."

"Then you are the goddess."

She shook her head, but she was pleased. Her legs were long, her body hair fine and blonde. Later, in her hotel room, he tasted her velvet recesses while she taught him to match her pace, but each time he thought he had mastered the point, she changed the rules and waited for him to catch up. She was nineteen. He was seventeen, and his youth taunts him to this day.

———

SO MANY MEMORIES fill the cantina. Already Esquivel feels his weariness, and the sun has only begun to lay its stripe across the bar. He picks up his towel, polishes a glass, and sets it alongside the others. Tonight at midnight begins *El Dia de los Muertos*. Today, already, the ghosts visit his cantina.

CHAPTER FOUR

Corte: Cutting, as a cutting word

I n the cantina, the past explodes with a will of its own. Esquivel brings the Greek girl close, laughing and wringing the sea from her tresses, water dripping from her clinging sundress, in his mind, more erotic than if she stood before him naked. He steels himself while she pirouettes around him, holding his right hand with loose fingers then slipping free, nails trailing across the front of his trousers—not quite touching, but close enough.

He feels her heat across his left hand, but she doesn't meet his eyes, doesn't seem to notice his attempts to control the quiver of electricity. He stares straight ahead and wills himself not to respond, feels her playing with him until he thinks he will burst. Twice more she circles, coltish, then sylph-like, dances on tiptoe as she possesses his burning fingers, releases them, and moves on. He concentrates on keeping his arms loose, his hands relaxed while everything in him screams for her to stop the game, for her to take him with more than the pressure of her fingers. When she smiles into his eyes her guilelessness should have been a warning, but he thinks that such beauty could not deceive. This will be his first lesson about women.

It is this memory that absorbs him. When the smell of his sweat infuriates him, he reaches to turn on his electric fan and pitches the knob on the floor when it breaks off in his hand.

"*Madre de Dios!* Keep the door closed, woman. We don't live like the damned dogs."

From the kitchen, his wife shouts, "Watch yourself. You'll go to hell with that talk. Shut the door yourself."

"*Vaca.*" Under his breath. "Cow." Shame claims his tongue. His wife is a good woman.

Layers of grease, cigarette smoke, and dust dull the light from the overhead chandelier. It is Esquivel's pride, four small amber bulbs that together provide 60 watts, enough light for the men to see their hands, but not enough for neighbors to read each other's eyes. The white oak base of the chandelier is an ancient wagon wheel from Jose Orozco, the wood hauler's, oxcart. After the ox died at the age of twenty-six, the old man had no further use for the cart. A week before Orozco himself died, he bartered the wheel for a few days' worth of *pulque* and drank himself into a place where old men could still find purpose. Esquivel added an oscillating fan and taped a shiny *dinero* to balance the high blade. Now the coin is obscured by dust.

Tomorrow is the fiesta. It will be a bad omen to have the dust of decay in the room on such a day.

Esquivel's anger ruptures. Dusting is his wife's work, but she is short, and the fan blades are high, near the ceiling. One more thing for him to do. He grabs his bar towel and walks to a table still strewn with stale cigarettes and beer bottles from the previous night. He picks them up in both hands, using his chin to balance the load because he has forgotten his tray and sees little reason for making a trip back across the room.

A fly buzzes through the open doorway. It circles, grazes his ear, and settles on his eyelid.

"Get out of here, *hijo de puta*! You, I don't need. I got all the irritation I can stand. *Vete!*"

The fly circles and lands on the bridge of his nose. Esquivel's hands are filled; he can only shake it off while the fly rubs one leg against the other and remains. It tickles his nose and he swats his cheek with the back of his left hand. With the armload of bottles, his aim is off. He stiffens. Bottles slide when the fly explodes into his nose and his sneeze sends spittle through the room, dislodging his dental bridge. He grabs for a save and remembers the bottles, too late.

"Sonabitch!" Dregs of flat beer spackle the shards of glass on his new designer boots while bottles shatter across the tiles. "Sonabitch!"

He throws his towel and catches the edge of a half-filled water pitcher that dumps onto a stack of receipts piled next to his calculator. "Sonabitch!" This time, his voice raises an octave.

The stench of cigarettes in stale beer frenzies the fly.

Esquivel glares at the hook where the flyswatter usually hangs, but it is empty. He grabs a towel for the spilled water while the fly crawls across the back of his neck. He cuffs and misses. His boots grind onto the tiles, embedding glass into his soles. He turns in a clumsy circle and waits, but the heat has energized the fly. He tries to track its flight, but his eyes are not what they used to be. When the fly flicks against a window, he strikes, leaving the glass smeared while the fly buzzes off. He pursues, but his anger steals his edge. As the fly glides above the fan and lands, Esquivel sees his chance. Climbing a table, he straddles a puddle of beer and flicks the dusty blade so that the chandelier swings away. Esquivel slices his hand on the raw edge, but his yelp dies abruptly with the realization of what is about to happen. As he loses his balance, he curses the landing. It will be hard.

His face hits the table, and pain racks his vision. For a dozen seconds, he lies dazed, trying to breathe while warm beer wicks across the right side of his face. His dental bridge has sliced the inside of his cheek. Fire fans across his rib cage, through his chest, to his heart cavity, and fear manifests in the sweat dripping down his temples. In the silence, he hears the fly buzz back through the open door.

His roar of fury is his only payback for the last five minutes. "Aheeee!"

He concentrates on not blacking out and realizes he is a fool. Cheek-deep in spilled beer, he sees the remaining days of his life stretch before him, dry and shallow like the riverbed in the arroyo. Is he a man to hunt down wild dogs? Pain slams his temples. It is good his wife is outside with the chickens; she would only interfere.

But he is wrong about this as well. She is standing at the doorway, arms crossed, a flyswatter in her hand. The exasperation on her face fuels his anger. "Get the hell out of here, woman! Leave me alone!"

Wordlessly she turns and slams the door behind her.

He fingers the swelling bruise on his cheek. The thought occurs to him that he should have demanded a piece of ice, but now it is too late, she has missed her chance to be useful. But it is her fault—all of this—for leaving the door open, for being short, for not dusting the fan, maybe for being in this cursed desert in the first place. She was not the one he would have chosen—the knowledge has grated on him nearly every waking hour of his life.

His cheek throbs. He picks up the wet towel and wipes slivers of glass from his boots while his belly boils with indigestion. He glances over at the fireplace and sees the crumpled page on the cold ashes. Without warning, his throat convulses in dry heaves.

He sees the girl again, her dress falling around her ankles before she reaches for him, and he squeezes his eyes with shame at what he has become. For thirty-five years, he has managed to hold on to her memory, even the ache. Each year, when the vendors arrive with their lug boxes of peaches, he chooses one and waits until morning. In the dawn, he lets the juice drip onto his naked chest while he pulls the skin away with his teeth. He feels the velvet with his tongue, and he chews slowly until the juice mingles with his chest hairs and drips to his trousers. When he is finished, he rubs his hands against his skin, tips his head back, and roars like the jaguar in the hills.

———

THE CANTINA IS EMPTY. The silence leaves him with nothing except the pain—and her ghost. The hours will drag until the night brings justification to slake his thirst. Tonight, he will make a fire with the page from the magazine.

But pain has fueled memories. In his head, he sees the flowing script of her poetry. He remembers the poems, stuffed in a cigar tube that she left in his sleeping bag as though her words would be enough when she was gone. But he knows the truth, even if she didn't say as much, that his inexperience was the cause. She lied when she said it was not. In the cantina, his anger flares anew as he remembers.

"Don't go."

"I have to—my father expects me."

"Tell him it's impossible." He swallows and hears her low laugh.

"You're the impossible one. You will forget all about me."

How could she say such a thing? The pain still visits him in the night. She came to say goodbye. He heard her calling, but he refused to give her satisfaction. The boy he had been only a day earlier would have flung aside the leaves and revealed his hiding place, allowed himself one last time with her. Instead, he waited in the shadows until her voice faded, then followed her back to her hotel. When she willed him to look at her through the window of the white Ford taxi, he pretended not to notice and told a joke to the bellhops, one he had practiced so they would laugh when he told them the punch line. When she turned to stare from another window of the moving taxi, he pressed his attention on a shy girl standing nearby. When the taxi disappeared into the night, he fed his anger, hoping it would grow into hatred. But in his throat, it tasted like fear.

Tequila helped. He drank until he could not recall anything except her face and the smell of her skin. When only a few drops remained, he hailed a bus without noticing its route. As soon as the bus turned from the town onto the highway, he knew its destination: north to Chihuahua.

———

IN THE CANTINA he fingers his bruise and recalls mornings when the ocean was the temperature of his skin, and he could not tell without opening his eyes where the water ended and the air began. He keeps a thermometer and makes a point of watching when it reaches twenty-one degrees Celsius—the perfect temperature. But he doesn't need the thermometer. His skin tells him each morning when he stands naked in the yard.

He chose Casa Corte, not the other way around. He seizes the thought to remind himself that he has not always been the fool he is today. But regardless, he and the bus driver were not *simpatico*. Every bus that pulls up in front of his cantina brings fresh shame for the day he arrived.

CHAPTER FIVE

Corte: Cut down, interrupt

I n the bus, the little boy and girl did not look up. Their mother, in the seat across, glared at him as he slipped the cigar tube from his pack, pulled the sheets from inside, and tossed the lid on the floor. The poetry was all that remained of the girl. Written on thin pink paper, it tore easily into a pile of confetti that filled his palm. A gust of wind snatched them up and deposited pink squares in the children's ebony hair. Their laughter irritated him, and he pitched the cigar tube at the windshield.

The metal *thunk* startled the driver from his daydream. "Hey *hombre*...you start trouble, I kick you off. In this desert, you die before an hour."

He shrugged and turned to the window. Outside, a brown-skinned girl ran alongside the bus, one of a trio of Tarahumara Indians loping in a steady gait toward the next town. She looked to be about thirteen, with thick braids that glistened in the sun and high budding breasts mounded beneath her cotton blouse. She glanced up just as the bus passed, and her smile sliced fresh anger through him. He glared at the driver and made an obscene gesture with his middle finger.

The driver caught it in the overhead mirror and warned with his eyes that there would be consequences. But he sneered at the driver's challenge. Pulled his straw hat low and closed his eyes. He was almost asleep when the rubber of the recapped tire ripped loose and slammed into the wheel-well.

"*Madre de Dios!*" His hand broke his fall against the seat in front of him. He was not startled, only dizzy from the drinking. It only looked that way to the other passengers because he checked his pockets for his money. The woman in the seat across screamed for her children to be still—even though she was the only one making noise. He snarled at her to shut up as the driver downshifted and the bus ground to a stop.

"Get out, you *peon*." The driver started yelling before he finished opening the door—as though the flat tire was Esquivel's fault. On his way out, he remembered laughing. For the disapproving passengers, he pretended to be drunker than he was as he staggered down the aisle.

The dry heat hit with the force of a blow. Before he cleared the bottom step, the bus driver threw the bus into gear and lunged forward a few feet as though for the purpose of catching the shade of a pepper tree, but his grin told Esquivel that he was a hothead. The movement threw Esquivel against the bus. He straightened himself cautiously, not wanting to give the driver satisfaction. His head reeled. How many days since he had eaten? If he passed out, he would die, like the driver said, in an hour. Maybe this was his fate. He fished in his pack for the tequila, drained the last drops, and tossed the bottle into the weeds.

A hand-painted sign dangled from a piece of wire on a post: Casa Corte. *Corte*, for cutting, like the heat that seared his nose. He read the words again and studied the few shacks with new interest. Casa Corte was angry in a way that he understood. Hot and dry, it suited his idea of hell. Nearby, a sandy courtyard defied the heat because there was nothing left in it for the sun to kill.

On the day he arrived, the Indian girl from the road drew water for him from the well at the base of a gnarled pepper tree near the Plaza Corte—water that tasted better than tequila. She didn't say much, only that her name was Maria Juanita and that she came from the arroyo south of town early in the mornings to sell her family's jewelry to the tourists. She was not Greek, and that was enough. Maria Juanita had good teeth, and nothing about her reminded him of Acapulco. He made up his mind that he would ask her to marry him when the time came, and the shy look in her eyes told him she would say *yes*.

When he first arrived in Casa Corte, he thought it was not a village to waste water on flowers. Now, a pepper tree shades his yard—probably the seed of the tree at the highway. He was wrong also about the flowers; a leggy red geranium sprawls outside his front door in the shade of a bench, home to a skittish lizard. A half-dozen concrete benches line the patio for the nighttime when the heat grows forgiving.

———

IN THE CANTINA, Esquivel reaches for another glass and begins polishing.

CHAPTER SIX

Corte: To put on airs

I n the west, the Sierra Madre spreads her bony carcass along the corridor between the desert and the Pacific Ocean. By four o'clock, the blooded sun settles behind olivine-encrusted arroyos, sending long fingers of sunlight to warm the deep blue Mexican tiles.

The afternoon light picks up the gray in Esquivel's beard. He tries to compute the number of sunsets he has seen reflected in the sheen of his counter, he multiplies three-hundred-and-sixty-five days times thirty-five years. In his head, this works out to over ten thousand. A high number. And tomorrow another feast day.

Already, fireworks are offered for sale in the plaza to summon the spirits of the departed after the priest leads the procession from the church to the graveyard. The children will carry the candles past the cantina, laughing and dancing alongside the marching paper maché skeletons. Afterward, families will picnic on suppers of tamales and *horchata.* They will suck sugared candy skulls written with the names of the children. They will sing and tell stories, bathed in the glow of paraffin candles placed on the graves so the spirits of their loved ones can join the celebration.

Esquivel thinks to join them this year. He has no one to mourn, no one buried in the *cementerio,* but the young men of the village consider him an elder now. It is his duty to close his doors for a few hours and join in the storytelling. They hear his words as something worth remembering—the young boys, especially. They sit at his feet, listening to every word. When they are old, they will remember, he thinks. It is good, passing on the stories. These are his children.

A few men straggle in from their pickup trucks and battered Chevrolets, coming to wet their throats with their *compadres.* Sometimes, on summer nights, they sit outside beneath the tree, and their songs and their laughter carry to the neighboring houses. No matter that the noise grows loud, his neighbors do not complain because the sound is often better than anything their wives can offer. The men, they cool their blood together. There are no secrets in the town.

At ten o'clock, the moon rises, the cantina fills, and Esquivel remembers the promise made to his neighbor in the early hours. Maybe this night will end early and the men will return to their houses. When the room is empty, he will take his ancient shotgun from its hiding place and meet his neighbor to track Mendoza's wild dogs, the *perros locos* that run loose. But maybe it is not to be. Some nights, the men drink late, repeating stories that are very old, a ritual as soothing as the liquor.

Their conversation is marked with gruff laughter and jokes about whores and boils, but they do not probe the hunger that lies underneath. They will laugh when a *compadre* breaks wind or drinks until he stains the front of his trousers, but they will not probe. Neither will they hurry off. On the nights when they linger, it is as though the universe ends at the cantina door. He will hunt when the hour allows; there is time enough to find trouble when the drinking is done.

Sometimes, the priest from San Lázaro joins them when he finishes with the women at the mission chapel who line up for confession, their dark *rebozos* draped across their foreheads to hide their guilt. He is gentle with the women, patient and detached, but he doesn't offer advice. He tells them that God is pleased with their laughter. The priest knows they come so that he will lecture them on their wrong thinking and assign them penance to make their conscience right with God, but it is hard for him to find fault. He does what he can.

The women of Casa Corte are of two kinds, those who have no need to see what lies behind the doors of Esquivel's, and those who sleep upstairs until they are summoned to add a few *pesos* to their rawhide sacks. Only the first will concern themselves with the hour of their man's return.

Tonight, the priest drinks alone at a table, as he does every night.

Esquivel studies the priest and the thought forms in his mind that perhaps he should join the line of women and give his confession. But just as quickly, the thought disappears. He will take responsibility for his life. The priest offers no example to follow. Besides, the priest is not human; he has no need of women, but Esquivel thinks of little else. What good will it do to confess? He will save his effort for when his sinful thoughts are all that remain. Maybe God will see the irony in giving a man such strong desire and a cold wife who drives his need inside his head where it will not bother her.

The cantina is small, its crude pine tables set close. There is no space for chairs, and wood is scarce in the desert. Small concrete benches clutter the room. Backless, they seat a man until he has had too much to drink. On a bench, a man will fall forward, not backward, where he might hit his head on the concrete floor. Already, the air is dense with the smoke of the men's cigarettes, so thick it gives a taste to the tongue. Esquivel has learned to ignore it, but his wife finds the odor offensive. She has a fondness for the mountain air and the scent of the river. Sometimes her scorn for civilization includes him. Nothing to be done about it. It is for her to accept the price of the income he provides.

Some of the men drink *cerveza*. Others drink a local brew, *pulque*, made from the pulp of the *maguey* cactus and fermented in wooden vats until the liquid is frothy and filled with vengeance. Then, it is strained and poured into pottery jugs that he keeps under the bar, covered with cotton cloths he has brought from Durango.

The *pulque* is green at first. It will give a bellyache to anyone who drinks. It will make them wish they had seen the priest beforehand, but they won't die. In time, it will cure of its own accord and the drink will be better. Smooth *pulque* cures more than it harms.

Esquivel's cantina has the look of a dark, thick man with no concern for his attire, but there are two exceptions that draw the eye past the clutter of tables on the plain concrete floor. In the corner, a hint of color shows the hand of Esquivel's woman. It is a Christmas cactus she has nurtured through the summer months. During December, it will bloom for a few days, and then the crimson blossom will disappear.

Pancho Villa glowers from a dingy photograph on the far wall, his chest weighted with *bandoliers*. The men at Esquivel's have heard stories from their fathers and grandfathers of fighting alongside him in the mountains when the old men guided him through arroyos as familiar as the veins on the backs of their hands. The photograph is old. It was carried in the saddlebag of one of his *Villistas* for many years. One day, the old man's son stalked into Esquivel's, hung it on the wall, and left without saying a word. The men salute Villa's memory with *pulque*. They brag that their fathers traveled to Chihuahua to pay their respects to his widow at her *villa* before she died. Now the young ones go to see the bullet holes lodged in the old Dodge touring car in which Villa died on the dusty streets of Parral.

Had Esquivel's cantina been standing at the time, Pancho Villa would have stopped for a drink. The men agree. The *jefe*'s spurs would have clinked across the threshold. He would have seated himself on the bench where the men sit tonight. Eaten frijoles from Juanita's pottery bowl. "Freedom is a good thing," he would have said. "*Libertad* y *pulque*." Liberty and whiskey. The men can feel his presence. In the dim light, the photograph stands for something—the men agree on this when they are drunk enough to argue on the matter.

———

THE STENCH of sweat and rancid lard is strong in the cantina. The kitchen door swings open, and Juanita carries chicken *mole* from the kitchen. When she is done, she disappears. Her work is over, and she is glad to retire to the room in the rear, to wash the filth from her body with manzanilla soap and to crawl into her nightclothes. A room filled with stinking men is the concern of her husband. If he needs her, he will shout.

"*Buenas' amigo. Que tal?*"

"*Lo mismo como siempre. Y tu?*"

The door swings open, and a figure glides through, moving stealthily, like the mountain lion. It is Mendoza, a cruel-eyed *mestizo* from Alamogordo.

Esquivel appears to notice nothing, a skill he cultivates to prove to himself that he is better than the men who drink at his tables, but his blood chills. Tonight, Mendoza wears a silk scarf around his neck like a boast. It is the color that draws Esquivel: yellow, like the gold Mendoza guards at the Juarajeta Mine in the canyon—a case of the lynx guarding the henhouse. Mendoza's filthy gray trousers are flat where he carries his money; he is not here to drink. Something else causes concern. The sheath on his belt holds a curved fighting knife. This is a bad sign, a threat made worse by the storm that hangs outside the cantina door.

Tonight, the earth is bathed in the darkness of the hidden moon. It is the man's time, the time of hunting and stealth. In *la luna llena*, the full moon, the earth belongs to the women, a time of fertility and rebirth. Darkness challenges the dominance of men where only the cunning thrive. Esquivel does not like the mix of men at his tables tonight. The drinkers are not *simpáticos*; the thought worries him. Friends are good for business, but strangers can become friends or enemies in the toss of a coin, risky business that a bartender must know.

Mendoza makes his way to his table, where a young Indian boy sits beneath the photograph of Pancho Villa. "You die," he says. The command is less spoken than growled. The boy scrambles to obey. Mendoza is a malcontent, a man who picks at his own scabs so they will not heal. He is a man who lives in the bowels of anger and hard drinking—and in thinking of ways to cheat those who cross his path. He brings his knife from the sheath as soon as he sits down and begins to pare his fingernails on the tabletop.

Esquivel makes a fist of his anger, but the defacing of a table is a cost he will accept. The other Mexicans eye Mendoza with the caution they would give a surly dog. The insult is not lost on Mendoza; he slices the silence with his scorn.

"Someone has a problem with my dogs, I hear. Hey, Esquivel, amigo...you know anything of this? We need to fix this little problem before it gets bigger. *Comprende?*"

Esquivel keeps his eyes on the glass he is wiping, but he feels the hair bristle on the back of his neck. He struggles to keep his hand from trembling—a sign Mendoza watches for—and shakes his head as if the question has been merely tossed into the air.

Another man enters. He salutes Esquivel with the indifference of friendship. "*Quiubole, mi amigo.*" He ducks to avoid the low-hanging lamp. Lázaro Quezada is a friend, more Spanish than Indian, high-cheeked, tall for his race, and slender, with straight dark lashes and full lips that draw the eye. His presence tonight is a surprise. Usually, he has little time—or need—for the company of men. For him, life finds a path to *his* door. Tonight, he is restless. Unhappy. A woman is the cause. They have spoken of this many times. His friend has reached an age to settle down. Life is uncertain. No man can expect things to be easy forever with beautiful women and their gifts. Lázaro is a good friend, but he is spoiled. Perhaps he has come to seek advice.

Near Lázaro, the Indian boy stares out the window in the direction the afternoon bus traveled, as though he waits for the driver to return. He travels south to the Yucatan. Esquivel does not need to be told this; he has seen enough other young men with the same look to know. This one is small and wiry—the build of a field worker—with a slight scar under his left eye. His youth contradicts the worry in his eyes; he has seen much in his years, but it is his nature to accept his fate. This should please the priest who sits at the next table.

The young *indio* notices the food on the bar and pulls a few folded bills from his pocket.

Esquivel moves his attention to another man, the priest—even though he does not dress like one. He leaves his cleric collar hanging in the vestibule of his small church and pretends he visits in order to study the ways of men, but his fingers are familiar with the cup in front of him. He is a man who has traded his dreams for something that gives him less comfort. Esquivel knows this; he has sold him such comfort on other nights.

They are *compadres* of sorts, if only because they can no longer count the years that have passed since they made acquaintance of each other. They are the best sort of friend, the kind to take the other as he is and ask no more. This priest has studied in Mexico City and in Rome. It would be easy for him to maintain an illusion of superiority, but this priest from San Lázaro does not put on airs. It would be hard if he tried—the men know his history. They make allowances, but only because he does not hold himself up.

CHAPTER SEVEN

Corte: Cut off, as from a crowd

At the bar, an old *americano* quietly sips *pulque* from a clean glass, ignoring the chatter. His ten-year-old, black Mercedes sedan squats in the sandy yard—so he has come from money, but he has none now. His discolored *huaraches* and baggy linen trousers give him the look of a man who conducts business in Mexico with regularity. Perhaps he is an engineer searching for a mine. Perhaps he plans to dynamite the arroyos in Casa Corte so rainwater will leach through the tailings and make the water fit only for cacti. When he is finished, drinking water will have to be trucked in. But engineers don't wear sandals. Maybe he is one of the gringos who come to retire, an expatriate who buys an old colonial house in a forgotten town, then goes native and hedges his bets with *pesos* and American dollars.

On second glance he looks like a professor of college, a man for whom words have rhythm. Like a dance.

The *americano* is weary of watching the moonlight. He stares into his glass with a detachment that doesn't invite intrusion. His face is bloated. His eyes, deep-set and guarded, are the color of the sky on a hot summer day. He slumps from more than the lateness of the hour, as though failure and success have conquered him, and he no longer courts either. Esquivel has seen his type; he drinks so that night will bring sleep. Perhaps he chooses his place at the bar so that the laughter is at his back. If so, he has chosen well. He is not a tourist. He does not travel with an eye to seeing new things. *This is too bad. He is a man who would know how to live. Perhaps he travels to escape.* A traveler with purpose.

Esquivel studies the room as he has done for thirty years. At night his cantina is not usually bothered by the gringos with their dollars and their requests for ice. For good or bad, the *turistas* do their drinking in the cities where the bars have air conditioning. His patrons are not wealthy, but sometimes, it would be good to have their money. To watch wealthy men peel money from their pockets. Plastic credit he would not take, even if every gringo heading south stopped to fill their belly at his tables. A man who cannot pay for his drink with the money in his pocket had better go home and wait for a better day.

Tonight has been good. He has already filled a cardboard box with empty Tecate bottles, but the men are drinking *pulque* now. It is a thing he knows—combining beer and *pulque* will make a man do crazy things. More than anything else, it is the weather that sets the mood. Winter is the easy time, when darkness comes early and earnest men return home to wives and children and the hot meal waiting. Tonight, Mendoza is here, and that is not a good sign.

The Zapoteca boy from Yucatan signals he will trade a

dozen pesos for a meal of Juanita's *mole*. He eats slowly, drawing comfort from the food. A boy who has been hungry many times in his life will eat this way, allowing his brain to tell his belly when he is full. In time, he will come to question all things, become slow to follow his passions, grabbing only what is safe. Something about him seems familiar; Esquivel has met him somewhere before, but he feels no connection. It is a hard world. The boy must make his own way.

This one is too young to be a lover. The idea is firm in Esquivel's mind—the boy needs a few years before he tries out a woman. His head throbs with the idea that the boy might be so stupid as to try. He takes a breath, and the tension releases. It is easy to tell about the older men, but this young one carries a secret.

He allows himself a closer look, but the boy does not raise his eyes from the plate.

Esquivel turns to the priest—another man to hold his secrets. The padre has the look of a Castilian, but his arrogance has been worn away by the road. He wears his hair short, nearly shaven—the set of a monk. His jaw is jutted, his flesh spare, as though he takes pleasure in denying himself. But he is not a penitent on a journey, a robe-wearer who fingers his beads, oblivious to the world. This one has lived among the world for too long. He walks the desert in search of his soul, following the example of *El Señor*, his Jesus.

Whatever his purpose, he does little to prove he is a priest. The women of the village complain that he scarcely gives a sermon at the Sunday Masses. But for all, his eyes do not condemn, not even Conchita, when she comes down the stairs on the heels of a man who has just finished with her. Perhaps the priest would like to follow her up the stairs. If so, he has never shown the inclination. Maybe he looks for ways to deprive himself—of everything but the bottle.

Mendoza. It would be a good thing if Mendoza were a stranger, but the fact is, he comes often. He gives the impression of a man who prefers his own company, even as he intrudes into everyone's business. He makes the atmosphere in the cantina fragile, like the air before an electric storm. His clothes bear the stench of many days. His hair is tousled and filthy, in need of trimming, as is his mustache. His eyes are strange tonight. He marks his territory like a dog pissing on the corner posts. He will bear watching.

Mendoza shouts without turning, "Hey, pinche! Turn up the music! What kind of place you run here—a church? The priest here would like that. He wants our money left on his table for his god. Well he can take a piss. My money is my own. No god comes to me and says, 'Mendoza, my friend—here is a little extra for you today.' Hey, priest, maybe your god sets us up with a round? Mierda!"

The glass Esquivel polishes explodes in his hand, but the towel hides the broken pieces. No damage done.

There was a time when Mendoza was not so bitter. When he was a young man, he donned a uniform and served in the army down in Oaxaca, where the Mixtecan campesinos labored to undo the erosion of the hillsides. He took pride in his country, but he learned that the money was in drugs. A man who possessed a steady nerve could go far, but his enemies required payment, sometimes more than a man could justify. He learned to live like the sly dogs, cautious and alone.

Although he came home a different man, the villagers held their opinion. He wooed a shy local girl who looked at him with such soft eyes that, for a while, many in the village thought he could be a good husband. But, in time, the patience of behaving well drained him of everything but an inclination toward cruelty. His behavior drove his wife into herself where no sound or gesture would unleash his anger, but sometimes even that was not enough.

The week she delivered in childbirth, she could not keep her newborn from crying while her husband slept in the bed next to her. His mood was foul that night, his dreams filled with the shrill squawks of parrots. He woke drunk and angry. The neighbors heard the sound of her screams, the thump and crash of objects hitting the walls. They thought nothing of this; it is a man's right to discipline his wife. But the next day, one of them recalled him shouting for her to shut the baby up or he would. When the baby was taken to the doctor with a twisted leg, the men in the village were afraid to act. When the women turned their backs on Mendoza, he allowed their anger to isolate his wife as well.

It was Mendoza who hung Pancho Villa's photograph on the cantina wall. One day, he strode in the open door with it under his arm. He drew his knife from a pocket and used the handle like a hammer to pound a nail into the grout between the bricks. When it was deep enough, he hung the wire across the nail, stared at the melancholy eyes of his *jefe*, turned, and walked back outside.

Esquivel glances over at the picture. Dingy from the smoke of the years, the photograph is signed by the *New York Times* photographer sent south to cover the war. This information came from a gringo sociologist who wanted to buy the photograph for his collection. Esquivel tried to explain that it was not his to sell, but the gringo still wanted to barter.

Tonight, Mendoza drinks beneath the photograph. Maybe he would kill for his right to the table, but it has never come to this. His ownership is explained in whispers and gestures to newcomers.

Beneath the bar, the black rotary phone rings once, twice, then again. Esquivel picks it up and listens. He nods without realizing he is doing so and hangs the phone back on its cradle when the line goes dead. "The rains are heavy in the mountains. Anyone who wants to make it across the arroyo better go now. The rest of us will be stuck here for the night. You see anyone, let them know."

In minutes, the cantina is empty of all but the ones who have nowhere else to go. The priest remains, and the *indio* boy. And Mendoza—he lives on the other side, but he apparently has lost his nerve to race the water this time. Lázaro remains as well. He has weathered the floods many times; perhaps he has nothing to rush home for. Or perhaps he has a need to be with strange *compadres*. Whatever, he will spend the night.

———

A BLAST of cold air threatens the fragile flame in the fireplace. Esquivel's heavy pine door creaks to admit a pair of cowboys—gringos even before they speak, from the look of their round-toed cowhide boots and their dusty Levi's. Mendoza's snort carries to the bar. The *americano* doesn't pay attention, but Esquivel watches without smiling.

The shorter of the two, blonde, carelessly unshaven, claims the room before the door slams shut. "Sheeet, man...you burning trash in here?" He wears his long-sleeved western shirt rolled to his biceps, a half-empty pack of Marlboro's twisted high on his right sleeve. So, he is left-handed. His sweat-stained straw hat shades his eyes, its brim rolled to a point in the front, the sides battered from too many landings on rodeo sand. *This one will be the brawler.*

The other one, dark-haired and handsome, glances around the room. *He is no threat.* Esquivel remembers him from another season when he shared drinks with Señor Leon, a breeder of bulls on a large hacienda just outside Chihuahua. But the dark-haired American is not with the breeder tonight. He has brought the small blonde tiger, a friend from the north. They make their way to a corner table, sauntering as though they expect to buy the room with their dollars and their charisma. Esquivel hears the blonde one address his friend and he stores the information for the time it may be useful; the dark-haired one's name is Jim.

Mendoza listens without looking up. He knows enough English to pick up the substance. One way or another, he will use the information. Right now, he sits alone and scowls from deep-set eyes closed into narrow slits. The Americans have already noticed him, but they have taken a wide path around his table. If they have need of directions, they will ask someone else.

They bring the smell of their sweat, a reminder that they work hard for their *pesos*. Another smell assails the room. Even the closed door of the kitchen cannot contain the wet, singed feathers and the entrails of the chickens Juanita has butchered.

The little blonde cowboy checks the room. "Hey, barkeep—we get a beer over here!" He drops a handful of *pesos* on the table as though there are a thousand more in his pocket. Esquivel nods and brings a pair of Coronas. He plunks down a half-dozen *limón* wedges on a brown pottery saucer.

The cowboy is excited, his voice harsh in the silence. "Sheeet! I seen some flash floods in my time, but nothing like that! Water came out of nowhere. My buddy's truck's got stuck in the sand." He turns to Esquivel. "Who drives that big Chevy parked outside?" No one moves. Through the smoke, he sees Mendoza watching. "You the guy drove right past us—wouldn't give us a tow?" Mendoza sits unmoving. "Hey, dude...you speak English?"

Mendoza takes a sip and replaces his cup in its water ring.

The blonde cowboy understands the insult. He takes a step forward. "Hey, Mex...what's up? You deaf? Ten more minutes there wouldn't been anything worth saving."

He is nearly upon the table when Mendoza speaks. "The river takes what it wants, gringo. Tonight, it wants your truck. That's okay by me."

The blonde cowboy starts, but his arm is caught by the dark-haired cowboy, who bends to argue softly in his ear. The blonde swigs the last of his beer and picks up his hat with an angry glare at Mendoza. Together, the two Americans disappear out the door.

Esquivel watches the men jack up the truck to change the tire that has blown. Outside, the river roars its vengeance on the desert as it carves a channel across the sand. But the town was built out of the river's reach. The flood of '84—sixteen years earlier—was the worst in his memory. A day earlier, the desert was a bed of *maguey* cacti and sand until the water came raging from the hills, laying open the desert like a wound. He joined the villagers the next morning to see for himself the fury that kept him awake for most of the night. For a half mile, the desert was gouged into a channel eighty feet deep, a quarter of a mile long. A pair of Cadillac fins stuck out of the sand. Further up the arroyo, three longhorn cattle protruded from the sand, their horns tangled together, already attracting the buzzards.

Tonight, darkness and the river claimed the earth. But

tomorrow, the water would be gone. Maybe he will find another Cadillac fin.

He is still standing in the yard, listening, when the men finish. He listens to their chatter as they find their seats. "You see that car behind us disappear? Cripes! I would have made it across the first time. Wasn't for that tire, I'd made it clear." The blonde cowboy slumps into a seat with his back to Mendoza, but his anger is directed over his shoulder. "Thanks for nothing, dude."

Mendoza utters a harsh, mocking laugh while Esquivel starts forward with fresh drinks. It will be a long night. If he isn't careful, the buzzards will gather outside his place in the morning. The dark-haired cowboy is generous with his tip. Esquivel feels the sting of embarrassment. "Not necessary."

The dark-haired cowboy shrugs. It is his friend who talks too much. "Take it. I need a real drink after that! Beer don't hardly seem strong enough."

"I got beer—and *pulque*. Take your pick." The gringo should be grateful he has his life and a warm place to drink tonight. By tomorrow, the road will be clear and he will be on his way. Some men, they always want more than what there is.

Mendoza is not to be ignored. "You American rich boys supposed to drink wine!" His laugh is grating, already challenging. His sneer curls the corners of his lips.

The short one starts to rise. The dark-haired one places a hand on him and toasts Mendoza with his bottle. His manner is sincere, not hard-edged like his friend. He understands that the night will be long and there is no need for tempers over something so simple. "Wine is like a woman. Takes the right mood. And I ain't feeling it with my friend here." The joke is lost on the room. His blonde friend waits a moment and settles back to his beer.

Mendoza is not satisfied. "Mexican *cerveza* puts hair on your chest. That what your friend's afraid of, Jeem?" The others draw their heads down. The Americans are silent except for the scrape of their bottles on the table.

Esquivel wipes the counter and frowns. It is the hour for trouble. Four against three, even though the priest will not fight, he will end up taking sides, and the Americans will lose. He tries diplomacy. He knows about wine, even though he has never opened a bottle in his cantina. "American women like their men to drink wine. Makes them romantic. You like a little romance, no?"

"Romance? When my money buys half an hour with a woman—that's romance! Hey, amigos?" Mendoza makes a lazy gesture toward Esquivel. "We stuck here for the night, I take some of those *frijoles* your woman makes." Juanita has disappeared for the night. His eyes register satisfaction at the sound of Esquivel calling her back into the kitchen from the back of the house. He tips his head to stare into the ox wheel candelabra overhead and goads him further; "*Hey, pinche!* Good thing the lights are low, *mi amigo*. This yellow *burra* from the *norte* is hurting my eyes. *Mierda!* He is too pretty for the room. You are right about one thing, amigo. We need some romance. Next time, you gringo boys send your sisters down here to spend your money. We like it when the pretty girls come to see us!"

No one laughs.

Juanita enters from the kitchen carrying a steaming plate. Mendoza tilts back on his bench and waits with his arm extended so that his lazy fingers brush against her skirt when she bends to the table. He laughs when she twists to avoid him. "Me, I take any woman I want," he boasts loud enough for Esquivel to react if he has a mind to, but Esquivel pretends not to see. Juanita's eyes have gone dead. She slaps the plate of *frijoles* on the table in front of Mendoza, and he adds, "Any woman like a dog—"

The kitchen door slams on Mendoza's boast.

Esquivel catches the tight, angry face of his wife, and his stomach clenches. Something has passed between the two. Later, he will speak to her—his rule about staying out of the cantina at night is for her own good. He returns to the kitchen and takes two plates from Juanita's hands. Wordlessly, he carries them to the cowboys and watches when they pull the food toward them and begin eating. He favors them with a smile when they show gusto for his wife's food. They know that *chiles* will cool the brain.

Overhead, the dust on the blades is streaked by the slap of his wet towel. Across the room, Mendoza spoons *frijoles* into his mouth as though he has better things to do. He eats only to feed his belly, with no appreciation for the melding flavors in a simmering pot. No appreciation for the cook. Mendoza processes his food like an animal. In a few hours, he will eat again without recalling his last meal. As he lights another cigarette, food hangs from his filthy mustache.

Esquivel's stomach churns as he collects the empty *cerveza* bottles and mugs. He adjusts the radio, grateful for the thin music that peals from the single speaker. Before the question of insult occurs to the gringo cowboys, he settles them into their next beer.

"Sheeet...can't you hold that blamed cigarette till we finish? Hardly see my plate!"

The cowboy is only letting off steam. A man who likes to complain. He scoops his frijoles easy enough— Mendoza's smoke doesn't seem to affect his appetite.

Outside, the roar of water can be heard a half-mile away, where the arroyo cuts the earth into two segments.

The food is a mediator for the tension in the room. When the men finish, he will need something else to turn their attention from the hostility that rides the thick smoke. The night is untested, like a colt that has not been ridden enough to know what to expect from it. In an hour, he will have the measure of this room, will know how the night will fare. But for now, he must find a way to temper the hostility without setting off Mendoza. He moves to the end of the bar and forces lightness into his tone that he does not feel. He offers an idea that formed in his head that morning.

"One thing I know about a man. He does not forget his first love. Every man, he carries the memory inside him. A free drink to any man convinces me this is not true." The room has his interest. Encouraged, he turns to the old *americano* as if the idea just occurred to him. "Hey, amigo! You ever have a woman as sweet as tequila at Torreón on a summer night?"

The stranger stares back for the space of a blink. Too old for this nonsense, he understands what is expected. Maybe he feels the energy in the air tonight and will give up the secret that is festering inside him. His eyes contemplate the possibility, then waver.

"Sure...I knew such a woman." The clinking glasses cease in the second it takes him to decide. "What the heck." He makes his decision. "I'll need another drink. Whiskey. Scotch. Women cause too much pain for *pulque.*"

Esquivel nods and pours another glass of *pulque.* With any luck, it will be a long story. The man will get his money's worth.

CHAPTER EIGHT

Hacer la corte: To court as a woman

"**O**nce I knew a woman…" The *americano* punches his stub of cigarette in an overflowing ashtray and fixes his gaze on the heap. He has emptied many glasses already and his talk flows smoothly. Without realizing he has broken off, he strokes the corner of his lip with a pudgy thumb. "She was everything. The kind of woman you dream about—fresh—the kind that comes with the night and is gone before your arms get their fill. She makes you see what a fine trap you're caught in—and you're ready to trade your whole life for a night with her. But when she's sucked you in and it's too late, she's gone. You wake up and realize it was just a cursed dream." He coughs, and a fine mist of spittle drifts onto the bar. He looks up for the first time, his eyes squinting in the gloom. "Only this time she was real." He pats his pockets for his pack of smokes, halts, and whispers, "She was real."

Cigarette smoke roils in the dusky cast of the over-head lamp, its glow diffused like the speaker's voice. Each man leans forward, even the priest. One nods. He has shared a night with such a woman. Esquivel polishes, turning the towel around and around while sweat beads his forehead. His eyes glaze as his own memories merge with the lost dreams of his youth.

The *americano* continues. "We talked for hours. About her life. About my travels. About the children we never had, the lies we never told, and those we did. We talked until all the words in the universe lay fermenting in our bellies like grapes, making us drunk with the punch of the new crush. There was a moment...you know the one, when you wanna taste the new wine. But you're afraid to tap the barrel because, if it's not ready, the harvest will be spoiled? That's what I thought when I saw her. That she was waiting to taste the crush.

"When she spoke...thought maybe I imagined it. But I'd heard right. 'Will you let me love you?' That's what she asked."

Eight men grip their glasses while the room devours its oxygen. "Came out of nowhere. She was one of my graduate students. Not a girl. Old enough to know her mind. I sat there trying to think of some reason why I should say *no*. I looked up, and she was still waiting... waiting for me to say *yes* or *no*. I couldn't get the words out fast enough. 'Yes,' I said. Only that. I said *yes*.

"She stood. When I didn't move, she pulled me to my feet, and I thought my legs would collapse. I couldn't support myself. Felt nothing. Everything. Tried not to think. I wondered what the hell I was doing. The ques-tion was in my mind, but I stood like a dumb ox and waited." Sweat pools at the corners of his mouth. He swabs his face with the back of his hand, once across the mouth, again across his forehead where fine stands of white hair plaster against the dampness.

The *americano's* words remind Esquivel of the lost *poder* that plagues him in the night when his dreams charge him with vigor, yet his manhood lays soft against his loins like an old woman's breast. The younger men would not know of this, but their time will come.

The *americano's* words come back into focus. "She slid her fingers along my forearms. I felt the hairs tighten as though they were connected to my...everything connected to that one spot. Heard myself breathing. Hard. Trying to keep my feelings hidden. You know?"

He looks up as if expecting an answer. It isn't a question, not really, but the men nod anyway, answering for themselves. No one moves.

"Her arms moved across my back, burning. A good hurt, you know? Like scratching an itch. She pressed her mouth here...where a woman knows. Slowly, she brushed her breasts against mine. Burning me like two coals. I wanted to touch her. Half afraid the dream would end."

"*No huevos!* No balls!" Mendoza mutters. He flavors his insult with a smattering of English to show he knows the profane words. He is uncomfortable with the intimacy of the room. No one pays him any heed, and he settles back with a grin.

The *americano* does not seem to notice the interruption. "She moved her mouth across my chin. Wished I'd used the razor that morning, or even the day before. I was angry with myself, afraid she would stop doing the things, but she didn't seem to care. 'Careful,' I whispered, meaning for her to not be sorry, later. 'I don't mind,' she whispered. Her words struck me, and I understood. She wasn't meaning only about the whiskers.

"She kissed my cheeks, my earlobes. Not my mouth.

And I understood her reasons. I stood there, frozen. She slid her arms under my shirt and played her hands across my back. The feel was fire and ice, a volcano when the lava hits the ocean. Every nerve wanting her. Her fingers found me. I couldn't hold back.

"So many thoughts. I wanted to take her someplace and press her against a mattress, but instead, I stood there. I heard her moan. Felt it against my skin. You know?" One of the men nods. "It was all I could think of. That she wanted me. That's when I knew it wasn't a dream.

"I tried to take my shirt off. As clumsy as a kid, I pulled it over my head, aware of the look of my body for the first time in many years. Not a young man, but I saw she didn't care. Her eyes made me proud of what I was. That was her way, you know?" The men nod. They know.

"I stood there. Slid my hand down inside her skirt. Ahhh...I had forgotten the feel of a woman's skin, her scent when she's on fire. I buried my nose in her hair and breathed. There was no part of her I didn't want. Maybe I mumbled my thoughts, I can't remember. I might have, knowing what a woman likes to hear."

The priest nods, his eyes soft. Such an oversight is understandable.

Esquivel feels the fire. The *americano's* woman heats him and he presses himself against the counter, eyes closed. But the image that drives him now is Conchita, the upstairs whore who pays him for the use of a room. He collects a portion of her income, and each time the weight of the coin burns his palm. Tonight, he imagines her drifting in the candlelight, masking in the disguise of the *americano's* woman. She dances near, and he can feel her heat until the speaker claims her once again as his own.

"My fingers, the backs of my fingers, brushed across

her woman's waist, hip. Remembering for my brain. It had been so long. I don't have to tell you everything— you can know the details. Enough to know that I was half-afraid. Hoping. I prayed I would have this one thing before she stopped me."

His eyes are black with the memory, even in the darkness, black. "Sweet Jesus, I thought my body would explode. She moaned—I remember. She ground herself against me and pleaded in my ear—something. I can't tell you what she said. But she told me with her body to keep going. Not to stop. I was crazy with pleasure. It was not enough to be standing in the light, wanting so much."

In the bar, the silence is broken by the humming of a neon Tecate sign in the window. Five men toy with their glasses, each man staring into his own private space. In the kitchen, sounds of rattling pans distract the men until the sound ceases and the kitchen is quiet. In another part of the house, a door slams. A log shifts in the fireplace and a cascade of sparks flashes onto the hearth, but no one bothers. The sparks burn themselves out on the cement, and the room is quiet.

The speaker wipes his face. Esquivel watches as the *americano* grows younger, restored by the memory of heaven gained—and lost. He is here tonight with coin for a hired woman. For Conchita. The act speaks of his story's unhappy ending.

"I wanted to see her in the light, but I couldn't bring myself to ask. But a woman like that—she knew. She seemed shy, but I sensed she'd been waiting for this moment. Why me?" *Why this stupid old man?* was the question he didn't express. "But of course I didn't ask. I should sooner have sold my soul." The *americano* rouses and glances at the priest. "There would be no hell for such an action, even for you, huh, Padre?" The priest winces and says nothing. "God understands. The pain after a woman leaves—that is punishment enough for any man, huh, Padre?"

Two of the men nod. Mendoza stirs from his chair and settles again with a fresh cigarette. "Bah! *Hombre!* You think too much."

"Shut up, Mendoza."

"He thinks too much. Throw an unpolished diamond on the gravel, can't tell it apart."

Conchita has slipped down the stairs and is listening in the corner, hidden in the shadows. Esquivel watches her without raising his eyes, without giving away his thoughts.

"Standing there, I could walk away and have a memory to last my lifetime. Where did we go from here? I was thinking I wouldn't get greedy. But there was no turning back. My thoughts were in both directions at the same time. No way to think.

"'Lock the door,' she said, and it gave me an excuse. So many years, I was thinking. Only that. So many years without a woman."

"You want, I get you one in thirty seconds."

No one takes notice of Mendoza.

"I looked up…her offering clear. We examined each other like kids unsure of our next move. That she had never done this before, I was certain. *Why me?* The question will haunt me the rest of my life. We were in a place where we wouldn't be discovered. I watched her eyes. The look in a woman's eyes." His own eye twitches from the smoke of his fresh cigarette. "I kept stroking her, knowing I couldn't do everything I dared. There were limits. I figured she'd be one of those women who would hate herself the next day, and me along with it. I didn't want it to be like that, so I made it in my mind to make it good for her. Better for her than for me, you know?" He hesitated. "That way, when she remembered. Hell, I didn't have any protection, anyway. What would a man like me need with some rotten rubber? It would have fallen apart in my hand after all these years.

"Lying there, I watched her. A woman quiet in your arms. That's some kind of feeling, huh? Maybe that's all there is." He rouses and notices his glass is empty. "Jefe... another pour." The room is silent except for the sound of liquid splashing against the glass.

"My mind was rolling in a fog. But I have it all stored. Up here in my brain. Feeling her body talk without using words. I heard it." He pauses and drains his glass with a hand that trembles. When he speaks, his voice is hoarse.

"I been loved in a lot of ways; some you'd need a book to figure out. But this was something else. I lay there, feeling her giving me something I never knew existed, and she had already figured it out."

A dry, hoarse chuckle rumbles from his chest and spills out into a moan, a cry like a coyote caught in one of Mendoza's traps. He slumps forward, his body racked with regret and ecstasy, nothing anything without the other.

Esquivel feels his blood coursing. He retreats inside himself to a place where he can hide. He watches Conchita when he thinks she is not looking, infusing the shape of her body against his own. But imagination is a poor substitute. He bites his lip to keep from making a sound.

"The thing is...when it was over, she cried." The *americano's* chin slumps onto his chest. "She had these tears. She never said why. Didn't say nothin'. Just lay there watching me like I was some kind of god. Man, I loved that. I knew I was never gonna have a woman better in my whole life."

The words catch in his chest, strangled by the phlegm of too many cigarettes and too many words. He makes a swift decision and gives up everything; "I never saw her again. I went back there every night for a year, but she never showed up. But it wasn't a dream. It wasn't."

His words fade to silence. The room waits, but he has finished.

CHAPTER NINE

Corte: Cut, as picked fruit; harvest

E squivel pours another glass and shakes his head when the *americano* reaches for his wallet. His courage corrupted by what he has revealed, the man studies his glass.

Among the Mexicans and the Americans, there is only silence. The men are bound by rules. They keep their faces hidden, but Conchita's eyes caress the *americano*, crossing the room without leaving her corner. Esquivel feels his gut knot with envy.

———

HE RECALLS the day Conchita arrived. She pulled a shabby valise from the backseat of a sedan and lugged it to the front door without a backward glance at the glowering driver as he pulled back onto the road. "You got a

whore?" she asked. He shook his head. "You do now,"
she said. "I get half. You won't have no regret. I make you
money or you send me packing. It's okay by me." She
started toward the stairs, the click of her staccato heels
loud on the hard clay tiles. Her thin dress swayed with
the movement of her hips, a distraction that allowed her
to gain the bottom step before the possibility of consequence occurred to Esquivel.

At the sound of a woman's voice, Juanita came from
the kitchen and listened at the open door while her *mole*
simmered on the stove behind her. Esquivel intended to
say something, but the afternoon sun caught the gold in
the girl's hair as she dragged her valise up the flight of
stairs. "Which room?" she called. When no one spoke,
she said, "First one is best. I'll take that one." Esquivel
had only time to shrug his shoulders before Juanita
slammed the door shut behind her.

The woman was right; the first room worked fine. The
one Juanita had long ago set aside for a nursery. Esquivel
bends forward to release the cramp in his belly. It is there
every time Conchita chooses a man—and tonight is no
exception.

Her story had come out gradually, over many
lunchtime meals *of arroz y frijoles.* She had been a bright
student through her school days, which ended when she
was twelve and went to work at a huge factory that
spewed blue dye into the Rio Grande in order to produce
stonewashed jeans for American teenagers. Two years
later, she looked better in the factory-seconds she bought
in the company store than most of the other girls she
worked with. The gringo college boys thought so, too,
when they came to Cuidad Juárez to prove their
manhood, and by fourteen, she had found a better way to
earn her living.

When her friend Flora disappeared one night, she tried to pretend Flora had met an American college boy who took her home to meet his parents. Three weeks later, when news of the first prostitute murders hit the streets of Juárez, she had many questions but few answers, *La policía* weren't interested in her opinions. It was years before the reporters investigated, years before American nuns led a demonstration for the girls who began appearing in shallow graves in the desert.

When her friend Desconcia failed to return one morning, Conchita packed her bags and headed south with an American salesman who was traveling south to Mexico City without his wife. When the friendship soured over a lewd act that did not settle well with her, she demanded he pull to the side of the road and let her out. Esquivel's cantina was a sign that God watches out for His daughters, even the whores. She did not know the fear in her face—when she faced Esquivel with her valise and her bravado—was what caused him to love her at first glance. That and her golden hair.

——————

ESQUIVEL WATCHES the smoldering ember of yesterday's fire. He hefts two fresh branches and tests their weight to judge whether they will burn at the same rate and adds them to the fire. Intense, like a woman, the olivewood requires vigilance. A consequence of age that a man becomes hard, the same with firewood. His wood comes from ancient orchards planted by the Spanish on steep slopes long ago. It grew slowly, catching sparse rainfall that made its grain grow tight and dense. But its season has ended. Faced with the slow rot of time and a last chance to be useful, the wood is grateful for the fire.

Esquivel feeds the flames while the *americano's* words burn in the air.

The night is cold. In the summer, the heat is alive, a demanding overlord that must be endured. Stifling and absolute, it is the determiner of everything in Chihuahua: the furnishings of the houses, rich and poor; the hour for rising and for sleeping; the pace at which a man works. Living is done with caution. In the back of a man's head, the heat is always a reminder.

Tonight, Esquivel is grateful. In a few weeks, summer will come, rushing, angry, and bullying on the very day the cool season ends. He knows better than to fight. Those who have tried have already died of sunstroke or melancholy, or they have moved north where the weather is more to their liking.

He, Juanita, and the ones who remain are strong. Small and sturdy like the pepper tree outside his door. Fierce like the Tarahumara, who travel from the caves and the remote *barrancas*, canyons, to play their music for the tourists in Casa Corte. Even on the hottest days, they come—barefooted and watchful—and they have taught him well.

He thinks back to the days when he first arrived, when the heat drove him like the hum of electricity in a high-power line. In a bartered room, he lay on a bed and dreamed of the Greek girl and her golden breasts while a restless ache anchored his limbs to the thin mattress. In the evenings, he could not pack enough living to curb his need. Some of the village girls were willing—those who were older and knew ways of protecting themselves. For a couple of years, he satisfied himself with these girls, but one day, Juanita appeared. He noticed the way the sun highlighted her skin, and he began to wonder if her breasts were golden, as well.

———

"HEY BUDDY...YOU can't listen to the professor's story. Your playing days are over." The blonde cowboy gives his dark-haired friend a light punch to the shoulder.

"Women are trouble. Keep them out of your head!" The words are Mendoza's.

"Good luck with that."

It does not matter who speaks, one is as good as the other because the words are true.

"Women, they are all whores!" Mendoza levels a stream of spit on the floor. "Their mothers teach them to hate men. Whores!"

The room is a woman, and she feels the insult. Esquivel feels it as well. The wrought iron on the windows is more than ornamentation. Tonight, the bars are those of a prison—he feels their squeeze like a man trapped. The shotgun is hidden. It is too bad the rains have claimed the arroyo. He could kill the wild dogs, and the act would ease his tension. He is not himself tonight. He is restless, in search of something that eludes him.

The cowboy Josh laughs loudly. Esquivel fights the urge to haul him across the threshold and kick him into the white sand outside. But he would lie there until sunup, and the coyotes are close tonight. Better he passes out at a table and his friend will carry him to their pickup. In the meantime, the two will spend a few dozen *pesos* more.

The other gringo ignores his friend. They do not look to be *simpatico* in the way some men are *compadres*. It is doubtful these two will watch each other's back. Probably rodeo riders on their way to Chihuahua.

The little cowboy's manner hints that he has no roots. He acts dissatisfied, as though the future holds no promise. No man would choose to cook his own beans or to have only his own company. A woman offers the promise of change. If every woman is like Esquivel's, she will see that the wood is stacked for the cooking stove, even if she nags until he does it himself. The thing about a woman is that she wears a man down, like the sea wears a rock. No matter if the rock is solid, one day, it will have a hole, and the ocean will pour through with each wave.

Esquivel's bruise throbs. Perhaps he should have asked his wife for a piece of ice.

The dark-haired cowboy turns to the old *americano*. "That was a good story, sir. It reminds me of someone. Maybe I'm just drunk enough not to care who knows it." He studies his wedding ring in the chandelier's light.

Esquivel understands the man's woman will be upset if she finds out. But maybe his blonde friend will not tell her. He suspects they do not get along, the gringo's woman and his blonde amigo. If he had to guess, he would say that each resents the energy of the other. The dark-haired one is a self-made man. One who basks in the energy of admiration. He surrounds himself with people who feed him, like the sticks that burn in the fireplace.

Maybe Esquivel is wrong about this man, but he has known others like him. This one has never been lonely. He chooses friends who are needy. Men who live in the reality of their own beauty have no idea what it is to be common, ugly, and scarred. The gringo does not notice the admiration that his friend gives him. Nor his pain. But a man cannot be faulted for taking the best of God's gifts.

If Esquivel had been given the choice, who is to say? The cowboy will tell a good story if he chooses. He speaks the slang of the Mexicans, and he knows the words for making love to a woman. He understands that Spanish is a language for praising a woman's worth. A poor Mexican has little else to offer, but he knows that a well-loved woman will make the days happy.

The Mexicans catch the cowboy's enthusiasm. They lean forward, all except Mendoza, who scowls as he worries a sliver of olivewood between his teeth like a toothpick.

CHAPTER TEN

Corte: Cut of the cards

T he hour calls for another story. It is the dark-haired gringo Jim's turn. "I'll tell you about the night I met my wife."

The *americano* doesn't respond, but Esquivel gives the cowboy an encouraging nod. Something to occupy the room.

Mendoza growls. "No one wants to hear about your wife, Jeem! Like no one wants to hear about mine!" He laughs low. "She so ugly she make gas in my belly. No room for the *pulque*!"

The priest's disgust plays on his face. Mendoza sees it and sneers. Esquivel has heard from Mendoza's own tongue that the priest comes to his house and demands he allow his wife and daughter to attend Mass, but the husband only laughs and slams the door. He follows the priest's angry footsteps and shouts after him, "You, Priest, have no *huevos*. You will do nothing." He likes to watch the fierce hope die in his woman's eyes when she turns away and resumes her cooking. He wishes the priest would visit more often. He has told Esquivel as much.

The sheen of Mendoza's skin reminds Esquivel of oil on water. Sweat runs down his temples, following the deep furrows like tracks through adobe mud. The man rolls the toothpick over his tongue as though it is a woman's nipple. He sees Esquivel studying him and exaggerates his tongue. Esquivel feels his stomach clench. *Just let Mendoza try—*

His thought is interrupted by the American cowboy.

"It was a Saturday night, same as any other. I'd been working on a ranch, but the foreman let me go that morning. I was flat busted and had about as many prospects as dollars in my pocket. Decided to head on home—what used to be home. Hadn't been back since my mama's funeral."

The cowboy Jim speaks quickly, with an excess of words that makes the Mexicans happy. His words are precise and clear. The young Zapotecan at the next table nods, his eyes bright. Esquivel studies the speaker. This gringo is not a rich man. American ranchers are no longer rich, most of them, anyway. There are two kinds, the ones who accept their circumstances and those who cover their pride until they owe everything to the bank. This one will hold out when the land developers come with offers of money. He will pass his way of life on to his children.

"I cut across Highway 166, east of Cuyama. Pulled up to the Buckhorn Café about sundown. Couple of cowboys were settling their differences in the parking lot. Close up, I could see one of them was Josh here. I wasn't in the mood for a fight. Thought about skipping the whole idea, but I was hungry."

Esquivel considers the bars he's visited. Cantinas like

his are hard to find. The tourists have enough gasoline, they have no reason to stop in the run-down places. People who live in the towns keep to their houses at night and watch TV. The rural life is dying in the small towns. Probably no work even for the whores.

"I parked where I could keep an eye on my horse. Figured to grab a meal and a couple of beers and ask around. Figured I might get lucky. When Josh here brushed himself off, I saw he was sharing a beer with a buckle-chasing cowgirl I didn't recognize. He asked me what I figured on doing. Hadn't given it much thought, but I needed a quick answer. 'Rodeoing,' I told him. Had enough money for a couple of entries. He didn't figure I'd do it. Gal he was with flashed me a smile hotter'n a handful of chili pods. Figured I'd better get inside."

He nudges his friend. "Maybe Josh here ain't the brightest cowboy around, but he's sitting on a family ranch promises to be his in a few years, and that makes him a real catch. He knows it. Figures it's his trump card with the ladies."

Esquivel studies the man his friend calls Josh. When he is older, he will treat the women badly because he will blame them for his inadequacy. Already his liquor wears hard on the edges. The men of Chihuahua are not tall men, but they don't need the liquor to lift their boots or to harden their manhood. This man thinks he is nothing without his liquor.

Jim is speaking again. "I didn't have a trump. My dad had his share of losses—family ranch included. When he died, we paid our taxes and the medical bills and ended up with 'bout what he started with. Mom kept the house.

"Anyway, I found a seat where I could face the room. Waitress brought over a cold one. I'm not much on beer. Not like Josh here. I was trying to figure out my life. I had an ag-management degree and four years of college rodeo with more good memories than I could count. If any lady flocked to me, she'd have to look hard to see my trump card."

The friend, Josh, interrupts. "His looks is his. Heck, don't he look like a country singer? His mother used to brag on that."

The dark-haired American continues. "I stayed handy until Mama died. Took her to the Methodist church every Sunday. Saw to it the house was repaired, her bills paid— least 'til the day I called my sister to arrange a funeral. Mama's dying came hard." He grimaces at the taste of his beer. When he begins again, his voice is stronger. "Spent the next year cowboying. Loving every minute of it. Like every cowboy I know—wish I'd been born a hundred years earlier. Guess that's why I love old Mexico here."

The Mexicans shift, their eyes pleased.

"Heard the fiddler tuning up with my mama's favorite, *The Tennessee Waltz*. I was sitting alone, trying to figure out how I'd gotten into this fix, a college degree in a dying field, a handful of nothing. Wasn't feeling sorry for myself. I knew the facts when I started and I wouldn't a changed a thing. Make no apologies for living close to the land.

"I saw the door open. A girl entered like she wasn't sure whether to close it or turn and run. Tried to catch her eye. Another minute, some cowboy would swoop in and she'd be caught for the night. She stepped into the light, and I could see her blue eyes from twenty feet away. Man, she was pretty. Her Wranglers skimmed the longest legs I'd ever seen, topped with a silver buckle the size of a pony's hoof-print. She was a cowgirl. Not the Saturday-night kind Josh likes. This girl was the real thing.

"Tell you something. She was wearing a pink shirt with pearl snaps. And eyes with the look of a filly that hadn't reached its promise." His eyes are soft with memory. "That's what I remember."

He tells his story with passion. He will remember it when he is old and can remember nothing else. A man who recalls what a woman wears the first time they meet, this is a romantic man. In the back of the house, Esquivel's wife is sleeping. Sometimes, when he climbs into bed, he looks at her, hoping to see the soft mouth of a young girl again, but her mouth has grown hard. He wants to see the girl again. In the morning, she turns away, preferring to scour the stove. What is a man to do when his wife makes an excuse when he feels for her in the bed? If there is an answer, Esquivel has not found it beneath his sheets.

"I remember saying, 'Got a seat here, Miss. You're welcome to it.' I sounded like a Boy Scout. She started over. Someone jostled her and her hat fell off. This mane of blonde hair flooded down her back, clean past the brand on her Wranglers. I thought my gut was gonna twist cleanout. All of a sudden, I believed in miracles. Heck, I was watching one happening right in front of me. I jumped up and pulled out the chair and then noticed the cowshit on my boot. Heck, I had better clothes in the truck. I hadn't thought about that. I hadn't even showered.

"She didn't say much. Old Josh was walking toward us. I shook my head to warn him off." He turned toward his friend. "I figured I'd kill him if he didn't get the hint."

"Yeah. I saw that look." Josh gives a mock salute with his bottle, his expression dark.

Esquivel is a good judge of a man's drunkenness. He watches the way the blonde cowboy listens. There is a sadness in his eyes, something hidden. Esquivel understands. There are days when he wonders whether God will punish him for the dissipation he brings to the men

—some of them good men who would not drink if they had to drive further south to find a place. Maybe Juanita is right when she says a cantina is no place for a good man to earn his living. It makes his wife angry when he says God is too far away to notice a poor cantina owner. If God is in Casa Corte tonight, maybe He is hiding beneath the table.

He brings another round of bottles. The dark-haired cowboy has a few swallows left in his. He is right when he says he doesn't drink much. Most men, they say one thing and do another.

"I couldn't think of anything to say. I think I asked her if she wanted a beer. Course she didn't. She was just a kid. Maybe nineteen. Twenty. Said she'd take a Pepsi if they had one. Made my way to the bar before anyone could claim my spot.

"I turned around, and someone was already trying. I threw two bucks at the bartender and hightailed it back. Went to hand her the glass. Touched her fingers. Thought I'd been hit by a cattle prod. Tried to make small talk, but she was pretty quiet. Heck, I didn't mind sitting there. Figured she could play me as far as she wanted. Here I was, a good five years older, and she was turning my brain to Calf Manna. I didn't even know what to call her. 'Name's Jim Patterson,' I told her. She said she knew. Can you beat that? She knew. Well I'd never seen her in my life. Would have remembered. 'I saw you once. At a college rodeo,' she said. I still had no clue. My face must have shown it. 'I was younger,' she said. 'My dad took me. I watched you ride. That's kind of why I'm here. To meet you.'

"Cripes, my belly was jumping sideways. What was this cowboy's dream doing in a podunk dive looking for me? I sounded cooler than I felt. 'Well, reckon you found me, miss.' Or something like that. She said, 'My name's

Jenna Taylor. Jenna Lux Taylor.' I took a closer look. Heck, I knew her. Knew her family's history for a hundred years back. Miss Jenna-Gol-darn-Taylor was the heir to a ranching dynasty that spanned whole counties. And she was here, looking for me? I sat there trying to think of something to say. I know what the old guy there means when he says his tongue was as hard as his pecker. I wanted to ask, 'Why?' But I got confused. 'How'd you find me?' I think I said.

"She'd saved the rodeo program. Someone told her I might be at the Buckhorn that night. Heck, if I hadn't been fired that morning, I'd a been in Bakersfield eating Basque food. What are the chances? I asked the only question worth anything. 'Why?' I remember her lips were moving, but nothing was coming out. But I heard enough. 'I need your help,' she said.

"Don't know what I was expecting her to say, but not that. 'Of course! No questions asked!' I'd a eaten roadkill if she'd asked me to. 'Daddy's dying. I made him a promise, and I have to keep it before he dies.'

"Here it comes, I thought. She was chewing on a strand of her hair, and I felt my gut crow-hopping. For some reason, I asked her if she'd ever cut it—her hair. She said she was waiting until she found her prince or something like that. She was playing with me. Heck, I knew it, and so did she. And I sat there, loving it. I started to say something, but she cut me short. She was almost whispering. I saw the headwaters of a tear. But I sat there like the old man says, like a stupid ox. Strangest thing. She told me her father wanted to see her settled. Now the old man wanted to meet me."

At the bar, Esquivel swallows. Like the gringo says, what are the chances? Surely God must smile on such a man. From the shadows, Mendoza's eyes grow cagey as he teases the tip of his scarf against his lip and considers what he has heard. The gringo is a rich man, richer than he looks. Esquivel will warn him later about Mendoza. The young *indio* boy can't hide his admiration. He shares the cowboy's idealism—such a woman should exist for every man.

"I figured this was somebody's idea of a joke. I thought maybe Josh, but he was still occupied with what's-her-name. Still, it wouldn't be the first time he'd messed with me. But this gal didn't look like she was playing. She looked scared. Josh hadn't even known I'd be there. Nobody did. I looked again and realized she was serious. She gave me this slow smile that promised a lifetime of surprises. 'You'll have to meet my father,' she said. 'When?' 'Can we leave tonight?'

"I sold my pickup to some kid hanging around, the grandson of the banjo player. He wrote me a check. I pocketed the money and hitched my trailer behind Jenna's duelie. She was grinning when we pulled out onto the two-lane, me driving, her scooting close enough I could feel her heat. She caught her hair back up under her hat, and I could see she wasn't through playing. 'You figure on trimming that golden mane of yours?' I joked.

"We been married seven years now. Got two little boys. I swear I saw one of them in her eyes the night we met. Think that's possible?"

The *indio* boy looks pleased. Some of the men smile at the idea, but with a woman, nothing is impossible. The hardest thing on earth to figure is a woman. It takes a clear head to try. Esquivel knows this better than most. No man is going to try at an hour when their brain is already muddled.

"You're a good storyteller, gringo," Esquivel says. "So you never got to rodeo?"

"Not for a living."

"Too bad. Rodeo tests the marrow of a man."

The gringo nods. "Eight seconds looks like nothing to a man watching."

Esquivel relaxes. This gringo is not drinking tequila chasers like his friend. Anyway, rich ranchers don't destroy bars. If they fight, they pay for the damage. The cowboy's name is Jim Patterson.

CHAPTER ELEVEN

Corte: Gracefulness in dancing

Casa Corte boasts of a bell tower. It is a happy thing for a Mexican village to have tones ringing before Mass, a way for the villagers to share news. Even if the bell ringer is late to pick up the ropes, it is the thought that counts. In Casa Corte, the Angelus bell rings the news of death, birth, and fiesta. The ringing of the bell is welcome. A time when each person in the village knows the same thing—until the moment passes and the people go about their business once again.

By two in the morning, Esquivel's bar thins to only seven, those who have no place else to go, or those who wait their turn for the woman upstairs. Some intend to spend their *pesos* on the milky drink that fills their glasses; there are times when *pulque* is more important than a woman. When they finish, they will stagger out the rear door and into the alley, slump against the building where the sun is trapped in the adobe bricks. There, they will sleep until the flies awaken them in the morning.

The young *indio* found the guitar Esquivel keeps in a corner, an old *guitarra* he bought in 1970, the morning after he paid six *pesos* to hear Julian Bream play Bach and Fernando Sor on classical guitar at the opera house in Mexico City. In the late hours, Esquivel learned to make the strings cry. He played for himself, but sometimes a girl would look at him with soft eyes, unloosen the strings of her cotton dress, and quietly offer herself in the stillness. Sometimes yet, he can make the strings cry, on summer nights when the air is still and the desert tries to steal his soul.

The boy's skill resonates through the air. He plays from his heart. Esquivel has played for many years, but never as well. The music is a tune he recognizes—the theme from the American movie *Don Juan de Marco*—a difficult piece, pleasing. The notes run through the boy's fingers, and the men at the tables stop to listen. Esquivel feels as though he is hearing secrets he is not supposed to know, but this does not stop him from listening. The boy moves his left hand lightly up and down the fret, making love to the strings, his eyes closed, his mind somewhere distant, lulled by *pulque*.

When the music ends, he chooses a melancholy rhythm, something from his village, or his favorite by Hector Villa-Lobos, a Brazilian piece. The boy plays as though he is plucking the notes from his gut. It is a fitting piece for tonight, its energy builds and waxes like the tides of the ocean.

From years past, the golden girl haunts the room, a ghost Esquivel cannot escape. He does not try, but neither does he invite her to stay. He has found a quiet place inside his head where the past is as vivid as the present.

Women, they think talking is the way, but there are other ways—the boy with the guitar has found his.

Conchita begins to dance. Slowly, she uncoils the long shawl from her shoulders, and her feet begin to move in rhythm with the guitar. Tonight she wears a long, translucent white skirt that shows her legs more seductively than her mini-skirt cut short to the bottom of her thighs. Her peasant's blouse gives her a virginal air in the diffused light, and the image brings a tremor to Esquivel.

The boy looks up and notices. She is waiting to be led. He changes his beat, and Esquivel hears his sadness dissolving. He has found a partner. Together, they begin the ritual of the dance, a mating ceremony, one learning from the other, offering and accepting energy.

Conchita has seen too much of poverty and men. Each has made hard use of her, but her character is open and unfazed. She does not hold it against life, the pain she has suffered. It is her spirit that Esquivel loves. She is not a beautiful woman, nor a shapely one, but her body is fluid and graceful, her gait smooth and drifting. In the daylight, he finds it pleasing to watch her brush her hair or pick a crumb from the table with a moistened finger. She does these ordinary things without thinking, in a manner that shows her grace. Her laugh is lively, her wit quick. She photographs poorly, but only because she lives with such passion that the photographs cannot capture her. She shows plumpness around her face, but the small men who work hard for their *pesos* appreciate the sensuality of her ample body. They would feel cheated with a small woman; they can find thinness in their own women if they choose.

Conchita snaps her fingers, working them like a pair of castanets, her rapid movements defying the eye. She grips the edges of her wide, white skirt and whirls it in broad waves over her shoulders, showing her brown legs. She has small feet for a woman whose legs are not thin. She keeps her nails painted bright red. Her naked feet brush the floor, faster and faster, pressing the concrete in small whispers, *whisk, whisk*.

Esquivel feels the weight of her in his man-parts. He has seen her legs when she squats on the stoop in the heat and gathers her skirts through her legs and into her waistband. But seeing them uncovered is not as tantalizing as the glimpses he catches tonight.

She teases, only to deny him in the next instant. He hates that he cannot hide his hunger when her breasts heave with every turn, loose and unbound. She opens her eyes to impale him with a scorching invitation, and he returns her look. He knows what she does. Normally he would turn away and pretend she has no effect, but her bright, flashing eyes, her flowing hair, clear skin—especially the curve of her waist where her blouse pulls loose —the whole is too compelling. She dances to attract a mate. In his mind, she chooses him.

Esquivel feels the surge of energy. He is a rutting buck hypnotized by the headlights of a moving car that is nearly upon him. His concentration is broken by a low, grunting sound at one of the tables and he tears his gaze from the girl. Seven men watch her, one who would cut the throats of his rivals. Mendoza's eyes glow in the darkened room. He is a rabid dog and should be put down. If he were a dog, Esquivel would have no hesitation. The thought does not disturb him as much as it once might have.

When Mendoza feels Esquivel's glare, his raw hatred burns a path across the room. Esquivel is the first to look away. He hopes he has not betrayed the fear he feels.

Conchita crouches, her hair trailing like the mane of a wild horse as she tosses her head to expose her neck. Her eyes glow with the wildness of a free creature. Exhilaration drives her, tightening her crests into hard walnuts. She raises her arms, and her breasts are nearly exposed, the blouse untied in front and gaping, clinging to one shoulder—only the moisture on her skin holds it tight. At the last second, she shrugs the blouse back before it can slip loose and Mendoza howls his disappointment.

The sound angers her. Her pace increases. She twirls, frenzied, as though she seeks to escape something—someone. In the dance, she is a *soldadera*, loading the rifles and shooting and loading and shooting until the barrel is hot and her hands blistered by the heat of killing. Esquivel has no doubt it is a man she is killing. Nothing else would consume so much energy. Her anger drives her to a tempo of madness.

From across the room, Mendoza acts as though he owns something of her. Esquivel feels his palms go cold and wishes she would return to her room. Mendoza would take pleasure in forcing his hand. He is in a foul mood. His curved *cuchilla* lies on the table—but he has been warned. The last time he went upstairs, he left Conchita unable to work for days—and laughed when the judge fined him twelve hundred *pesos*, less than a night's earnings from his fighting roosters. What he bought for his money was the satisfaction of making a woman cower.

Mendoza watches her now, grinning. Her dancing fills him with anticipation as he waits, letting her work herself into a place where she will need a man in hard, strong ways to break the tension building inside her. He uses his leer to feed the anger, to push her faster in the dance.

Above them, the ox cart wheel dominates the room. Esquivel snaps the light switch off, leaving only firelight to bathe the room while the windows grow steamy against the outside air. Heat radiates from the fireplace; the room becomes hot and still, like a bathhouse, while the humidity builds. At the tables the men sit motionless, their eyes devouring the dancer while shadows dance to the rhythm of the flames licking the dying logs.

With a burst of embers, the room reddens to the cast of a blacksmith's forge, shadowing the men's faces, magenta on one side, dark on the other. Esquivel breaks his glance from Conchita and sees the hunger in those eyes. Stillness absorbs the room, the stillness of Pancho Villa's men before their battle cry. He reaches for the switch, but his will is frozen. The cantina is *la bruja* tonight, the witch.

The room vibrates with sex. The men sit silent, unmoving, their faces tense as each calculates the chance for success with Conchita. She is unfazed, her anger banked in the power of seduction. She tilts her head back and laughs, the sound breaking like a cool wave over their fire-baked faces. Sweat curls down the old *americano's* temples. Esquivel feels something at the corner of his lip and swipes with his fingers, sees Mendoza do the same, and quickly lowers his hand.

The young guitar player takes his cues from Conchita as she undulates with the rhythm. His fingers slip up and down the neck of the guitar. Her ebony hair pulls loose from its ribbon and flows across her back. She drops her naked shoulder and tosses her head, stretching a hard, expressive neck to accept Lázaro's tossed kiss. The boy closes his eyes and tips his head back, and Esquivel sees the flare of his nostrils. Conchita's lips invite. She is alive, more so than Esquivel has ever seen her. He glares at the *indio*, angry that his playing can stir such emotion.

The boy builds the intensity. He drums the wood of the guitar with his fingers, sending a primeval message—and Conchita is there, making sure no one escapes. Even the priest is sitting up, alert.

One of the men begins tapping the top of the table

with the flat of his hand. Another takes up the beat until each—even the *americano*—is pounding the scarred tables. Her feet make no sound, but the men supply the sound for the shoes missing from Conchita's naked feet. The blonde cowboy drums with the tips of his fingers as though the table is a bongo.

The log in the fireplace shifts, sending out another shower of embers.

Fire glows from Mendoza's eyes. Esquivel's nerves grow numb with dread. His thoughts tumble inside him. He feels responsibility for Conchita, even if she sells her body to the same ones later. That she puts herself at such risk fills him with fury. That she has refused his money on two occasions fills him with an emotion that does not bear thinking about. He convinces himself he is doing his duty and nothing more. She is more alive than he has ever seen her.

Conchita begins to slow her pace. She is tired, and she has accomplished what she set out to do. Her feet slow, but her body maintains its hold on the men and they are not willing for this moment to end. Esquivel attends to what will come next.

Mendoza will not be put off tonight; he intends to be the first. Conchita has made it hard to deny the man his turn. In the corner, he is putting his money on the counter. For him, the liquor, the woman, everything will be better, knowing he forces his will. Esquivel will not give him the satisfaction. He hides a knife behind the counter for the next time Conchita screams.

Esquivel turns his back, afraid to show the hate coiling inside him. The radio is still on, its faint static adding confusion. He snaps the dial off with a hard flick. It was Mendoza who demanded the music.

CHAPTER TWELVE

Corte: Cut, as to interrupt

A door opens behind him. It is Juanita, her long hair tied in her sleeping braid, stray hairs escaping. She has been awakened. She, too, wears white, a loose-fitting shirt that she uses for a nightdress. She has thrown a shawl loosely over her shoulders to hide her shape. It is the anger in her eyes that keeps Esquivel from turning away. In her hand, she carries her set of stringed marionettes, puppets made by a woman of her tribe for her saint's day when she was a child. Sometimes she manipulates them to keep her skill. Sometimes, when she hears one of the women in her village has given birth, she retreats to a quiet corner and play-acts with her strings and her puppets while she hums a plaintive melody of her tribe. Sometimes she performs for the children in the village, but never in the cantina for drunken men.

Esquivel's foreboding goes beyond the toys she carries.

Without heeding the dancing or the music, she sets all three string-puppets on the bar, suspended from crossed sticks in her hands. Esquivel makes a motion to interfere, but Juanita warns him away with a sideways waggle of her finger, an emphatic, unspoken *no*. This is no wife of his, this woman who ventures into the room of men. She does not glance up, and he senses it is because she does not want to lose her nerve, in the way that a man who mines deep in the earth does not permit himself to think when he feels the rumble beneath him.

For the moment, the room has two dancers. Conchita still captures the men; the attention of the room is still on her. No one heeds the wooden female puppet undulating in jerky movements.

Juanita is skilled at manipulating wooden legs and arms. The guitar guides the performance, and the puppet becomes a miniature Conchita, stamping her flamenco feet in an unrestrained dance of passion. She wears a vermilion dress. In the glow of the firelight, she is aflame, whirling, kicking, tapping her lampblack boots on the counter, click, click, click-click. From Juanita's left hand, another actor enters the stage, a man-puppet, musta-chioed and grinning, clad in pencil-thin, pitch-black trousers topped by a milky shirt and a scarlet sash. His boots tap in syncopation with the female puppet. She advances, teasing with an irresistible offer, then with-drawing when he responds. For the wooden man, there is no winning. She gestures for him to approach and rebuffs him once again. She undulates, hands on hips, grinding her pelvis toward him until he opens his arms—then rewards him with empty air when she suddenly retreats. The play becomes a bedroom farce.

The little man grows frustrated. The female is coy,

flirting with an unseen admirer off-stage. The wooden dancer renews his efforts, dancing faster, posturing in hard, staccato taps that sound like rifle shots, his wooden face fixed in a ridiculous grin that belies his actions. Under Juanita's hands, the dancers no longer play. He demands, and she refuses. His feet stomp in angry clicks. He is fighting, his rhythm miscued, his feet slipping as he tumbles to the bar. He rises on one elbow, shaking his fist as the female dances, ignoring him.

Conchita notices that some of the men are distracted. The music breaks off, and she halts, her lungs heaving.

Esquivel is confused by his wife's actions. It is their rule that she does not come into the bar at night. He is not sure what her presence means. The look in her eyes is a warning; she is not here to play.

Across the room, the blonde cowboy salutes the new performance with his Corona. "Ole, *Señora*. Give the little *hombre* hell." Some of the others laugh reluctantly, the tension from Conchita fresh and hard in their bodies.

Mendoza shouts to Esquivel's wife, "Take your cursed games out. Beat it!"

Conchita tosses her head in triumph. She is not surprised they prefer her.

Juanita warns Esquivel away with another look. She manipulates the puppet-man so he rises to his feet and sashays toward the dancing woman. The young man watches, his guitar silent. In the dance, the puppet-man courts the dancing girl.

Another puppet dangles from Juanita's hands. This one is dressed in the loose garb of a native woman with a bright piece of fringed cloth on her shoulders. Juanita manipulates her so that she begins to turn in lazy circles, paying no attention to the man-puppet. The wooden man hesitates, unsure now that there are two. The Indian puppet-woman moves across the counter. Her dance is slow, lacking passion. The puppet-man moves closer, but she remains aloof. He preens past, tapping his boots in smart, staccato clicks, hitching his shoulders, then marching straight-legged, like a military man. She does not notice. He increases his movements, gesturing, hopping up and down and clapping his hands, whatever Juanita can do to make him seem foolish.

Despite himself, Esquivel smiles.

The wooden Indian woman pushes the little man back and he tumbles to the counter, then rises and tries again. Clearly she has the upper hand.

Esquivel starts to laugh. When he turns and sees his friend Lázaro watching him with a quizzical look, he folds his arms and frowns. His wife is up late tonight, and that is confusing.

On the counter, the man-puppet rushes to the Indian woman and folds himself around her, pressing her arms tightly to her sides. He is contrite. She accepts his attention with little interest, but she tolerates his embrace.

Suddenly, without warning, the puppet-dancing girl rises from the counter. Whirling and stamping, she beckons him with her movements. He is weak, wavering between the two. He waggles his hand at the dancing girl, but he does not move from the Indian's side. When the dancing girl approaches and shakes her breasts, he jiggles on his wooden toes.

The *americano* laughs and flicks a quick glance at Conchita, who pretends not to notice. The blonde gringo offers his friend a bet that the man will lose, no matter which woman he chooses. His friend does not accept. Esquivel would not take the wager either. Probably the only taker would be the young *indio*, and he has no *dinero* to waste. Instead, he picks up his guitar and begins to play again, timing his rhythm to the action.

Without warning, the woman-puppet leaves the

wooden man's side and attacks the dancing girl, tearing at her clothes. The two engage in a scratching battle that tangles the strings and loops them together. On their knees, on their backs, they roll and paw at each other while the man lies in a heap on the counter. The guitar picks up the pace.

The men in the audience chuckle. Mendoza shouts for Conchita, but she does nothing. Nor does Esquivel. He would like for this to be over, but he only stands with his arms folded and waits.

Finally, the fight is finished, and the three puppets lie on the counter.

Slowly, Juanita extracts the Indian woman from the pile. The puppet taps her way past the man and exits the stage, victorious. She has made her choice and she chooses to be alone. Juanita reaches over and picks up the discarded man-puppet, and he limps after his wife. But the imaginary door is closed. He stands alone on the stage and glances back at the dancing girl.

At exactly the right moment, the guitar finishes, and the stage is quiet.

The *americano*'s slow clapping is loud in the silence, but he is undeterred.

Juanita does not wait for her husband's reaction. She disappears into the kitchen and slams the door. The evening will grow rowdy again, and the noise will wake her, but she will turn to the wall and dream that she is lying in the ocean, waves lapping her naked legs. It is a dream that reoccurs in her moon nights. When her body festers with the hunger of passion—at the time of the month when the cur dogs outside the cantina gather at her skirts to harass her as she walks to the outhouse. She has complained to Esquivel about the wild dogs, but he has done nothing.

Esquivel does not follow. He has much to think about

in the shadowy room where darkness hides his features. Lázaro Quezada studies him from behind his hands.

Mendoza turns to Conchita. She does not resume her dance. The mood has been broken. The guitar is tired as well. The boy orders a Coca Cola, and Esquivel is glad for something to do.

The *americano* pays a price for taking his attention from Conchita to the puppets. She whirls away so that her back is to him. He stares at his glass and ventures cautious glances at her, but he does not allow his thoughts to show.

Esquivel knows Conchita. She allows the *americano* his illusion that he hides his passion well. It is the way she honors him. His story touched places in her that she had forgotten existed. It is for him that she dances. She pretends with Esquivel—teasing and causing hunger— because she is a woman. But she wants to press herself against the *americano* and watch his pupils dilate. Instead, she sits across from Lázaro Quezada and pretends not to notice the *americano*. Esquivel turns away, unwilling to reveal the turmoil in his gut. The cantina is not the only *bruja* tonight.

The witch casts her spell. "So Lázaro—when do you come upstairs with me?"

Lázaro smiles. "*Ojalá*, one day."

Esquivel relaxes. Lázaro knows her game; he will not take her seriously. The *americano* shifts and studies his hands too intently for any purpose except to avoid her. This pleases Conchita—he is afraid of her, and this brings her blood alive. The memory of the puppets is fresh. She understands what was said. She and Juanita speak a woman's language.

Esquivel turns to find Conchita waiting for him to notice her. He, too, pays a price for allowing his wife to intrude. She stares at him long enough that he understands what has changed. When it was time for him to tell his wife to leave, he did not. For Conchita, this speaks louder than the lust he shows for her dancing. She has no use for a man who does not speak with his actions. He has lost his chance, she tells him in the swish of her head as she turns away. She has more respect for Mendoza. He leaves no confusion about his intention.

CHAPTER THIRTEEN

Corte: F. Royal court; retinue

I n Casa Corte, the sweet language of *mañana*
suggests no ambiguity for those who speak the
Spanish of the heart. They understand the subtlety
between a promise of tomorrow and a disclaimer of
simply *not today*. *Mañana* has meaning for the tourist as
tomorrow, but a poor man has only this day. The rich man,
he can afford to dream with no fear that his money will
fail his desires. A desperate man can look no further than
this single hour, but a poor man owns what is his from
sunrise to sunrise.

Lázaro Quezada pulls a crisp bill from his wallet and
pays for his drink. Between friends, money should have
no place, but his face shines with satisfaction as he folds a
bundle of bills back into his wallet and slips it into his
pocket. Esquivel returns to the cash register and pushes
the drawer open with a *clink*. At the sound, Lázaro looks
up and they meet each other's eyes. It is good, the money

they bring to each other. Better still, the money others bring from outside so that their cash boxes don't depend on each other. There is no honor in taking a poor man's money for drink and for whores. Better that the customer is a stranger, his wallet flush with greenbacks. The gringos are welcome. If they can tell a good story, so much the better.

Lázaro is a laughing man from Mata Ortiz. He wears his hair long, with gray streaks proudly interspersed among shining ebony. His hair is his heritage from the people of the mountain. He wears it tied back with a cord of rawhide. His cheeks are flat, high, and bronzed. When he is old, he will wear the creases of the sun, but for now, his face is that of a young man, with eyes that reflect his soul. His thick, straight eyelashes fringe the deep brown of his irises. His eyes project tenderness in such a way that sometimes Esquivel wants to touch his cheek. He is embarrassed at his reaction.

The women do not fight their desire. They understand. They see what escapes the men. They see the loneliness in his eyes, his hope that one of them will touch his soul. Each understands. It is not because he does not love her that he cannot settle on anyone. It is because he loves them all.

At his table, Lázaro palms a pair of smooth stones, rolling them over and over with fingers stained with black manganese. His skill with pottery allows him to remain in the village of his birth, no small matter for a man whose destiny was to follow the harvests north of the border. He began working in the sugar beet fields, hoeing lambs-quarter and thistle with a short hoe, hoping to find another way to earn his living before his spine grew curved like his father's.

Back then, he and Esquivel worked beside each other in the beanfields, in the years before the villagers learned the secrets of the Casas Grande people. The old ways. It was the children searching for firewood who found the clay in the foothills. Once clay was found, villagers learned to make pottery, and this freed the field workers to be artists. Money flowed into the village, and artists stopped hoeing the fields.

Lázaro believes he was taught by the ancients. The old ones, he says, returned in his dreams to give the villagers a way to survive. Their native ability flows through the fingers of their grandsons. Maybe to outsiders, this seems impossible, but Lázaro knows what he sees. Twice a week, the brown express truck stops at his shop in Mata Ortiz to take his pottery to museums and collectors around the world. It is an honor, selling pots to tourists who travel through the desert to watch him work. Each time they leave his village with one of his pots still warm from firing in the *quemador*.

In the dim light, Esquivel sees the white clay, the *barro blanco*, beneath Lázaro's fingernails. Lázaro's hands are smooth now, like his own. No longer do their palms bear the calluses of the hoe. He has seen the women watching Lázaro Quezada work the clay—at first, the consistency of a woman's belly after childbirth, later smooth and hard, filled with the tension of promise. As nature allows the woman time to bond with her child while her womb heals, so it is with the clay. It must ripen before it is ready to be worked. A potter accepts this. The women understand. They watch his hands patting the tortilla of clay as it yields to his will before he places it into the *puki*. He is careful, respectful, gauging the heat and the weight of the clay. He does not hurry.

The women watch. When nighttime comes, one or another will visit the small room at the rear of his house to honor his hands in the only way she knows. Lázaro understands why they come. In the moonlight, their love-making is the blending of two artists for whom giving is the best part. No money passes between them. The gift is beyond value.

A sensuous man, Lázaro speaks in a way the women understand, even those who use a different language. Women come from Japan, Sweden, and France. In the languid heat of the small room, they feel the language of his hands while his tongue lavishes slow praise on their skin. They unbind his hair, taking pleasure in the coarseness, sharing the sensuality when he unbinds their own. In the torpor of the senses, there is no misunderstanding.

Esquivel studies his friend with a feeling of envy. To have such mastery in one's hands. It is a wonder that Lázaro has not sowed his seed into these women. Maybe he has a dozen sons scattered over the land, each one carrying his father's blood.

Maybe his friend's story tonight will soothe the melancholy inside Esquivel. If he does not find something, his days will stretch into tomorrow and tomorrow until he is old enough to join the others in the cemetery. But then it will be too late. Tonight, the others will hear his friend's story, but the meaning may be lost. They are simple men, some of them with incomplete understanding of a woman, and others who have no desire to learn—like Mendoza, no better than a bull. They expect nothing more from life but to rest, to eat, and to expel their potency in a burst of seed. That is how most men boast of their encounters. Maybe Lázaro's words will be wasted on them. Maybe not.

Esquivel senses his friend's need to talk. The drink was good tonight, the fireplace welcoming. Lázaro is relaxed. His words form without conscious thought. Some of the men at the table are his friends, most are not, but the mood and the liquor make them seem so.

Esquivel sets his towel aside and leans close, encouraging Lázaro to begin.

———

"FOR ME, a woman is like pure, perfect clay. My hands follow her lines, molding and kneading her body, feeling her softness becoming a pot of beauty. Time has no significance. Only feeling. I uncover her as I do the clay in the fields. For many days, I watched the river, waiting. In the anthills, I see dots of white that tell me where the perfect clay is buried. With a woman, it is the same. If we take our time, we share the pleasure."

He gestures. His long fingers play the air as if it is an instrument. Some of his listeners nod; they hear his music.

"When we are alone, the two of us, we have all the time in the world. I run the water in my bathtub and add a crush of lavender from the garden outside my studio. The time we spend is like returning to the womb. No haste. No reason. We open bottles of *cerveza*, but we drink sparingly. Strong drink, like Esquivel's *pulque* here, is no good. A man and a woman have no need to hurry their drinking. There is all night if we pace ourselves. A potter who polishes his pots with stones knows a lot about time. Am I right, my friend?"

Esquivel nods.

"I rub the *agave* soap over her breasts, her belly, her legs. The bubbles explode, losing their strength until only traces are left. My woman's skin whispers when I caress it. Her neck responds to my breath. She pulls her hair over her shoulder to free the ear lobes, waiting. Her lips whisper soft words, but I do not always know what she says. It is of no consequence."

His fingers stroke the belly of the glass, tracing the rim.

"A woman's skin will quiver when it is touched just so. If you don't believe this, watch for yourself. It is true, I swear. Along her neck, I follow the heat. The skin cannot hide a woman's secrets. The soft skin above her breast will show goosebumps when she is ready for orgasm."

If he were not a friend, Esquivel would think Lázaro is making this up in his head. How can a man know such things? When a man couples with a woman, he does what he thinks is right. If a woman wants more, what will stop her from saying so? His own woman would agree—she would have little use for Lázaro's nonsense. There was never a time when her body was the clay that Lázaro speaks of. Esquivel remembers her skin when their bodies heated the room at the rear of the cantina. But she has grown brittle. She would break into a pile of potsherds before she would allow his breath on her neck. Or anywhere else. What does a woman's coldness prove about a man? Nothing. The question angers him. Lázaro is filled with the hot air of his baking fire—with the cow manure he feeds his oven. Esquivel has done nothing to make his wife the way she is—cold.

Across the room, he sees his unspoken thoughts in Mendoza's sneer. The realization that they feel the same about Lázaro's story brings him up short.

"I knead her neck, her shoulders...work my fingers down her back, soothing her muscles."

So much is said between flesh. Even when lovers are without the understanding of language. A man's body is made to feed a woman. How else would a race survive? Esquivel polishes with his towel. Maybe there is something to his friend. An animal that is caged does not thrive. Even though it breathes, it is waiting for its death.

Maybe for a woman to be alive she must feel, must be touched, must be fed. What good are words when her body feels dead?

"Sometimes we play a child's game. She slides under the water, and her hair floats like strands of seagrass. I pull her feet onto my shoulders. Caress them while she squirms and pretends to be outraged." Lázaro's thoughts smolder in his eyes. "I like the scent of *agave* on a woman."

The men return to their drink. Much has been said— too much for some. They frown, thinking it is a woman's place to scrub her man's back. It is not a man's duty. Esquivel's face heats with shame. It is not the business of another how a man treats his wife. Lázaro has never married. He nibbles at the edges of a woman's good nature without tasting the bitter fruit that grows later. He should lecture his friend on a woman's mood once she loses the will to please. He recalls the early days of their marriage. When his wife cooked a special dish or called to him with her shy eyes, he pretended not to notice, even though, inside, he burned. It pleased him that she spent her time thinking of ways to satisfy him. The years passed, and her fire smothered, but it had nothing to do with him, simply the woman's way.

His mother had worked hard to please. Anything that would erupt into anger in the men she served. It didn't matter which boyfriend, the only thing that changed was the method. Some men preferred a backhand that would knock her teeth loose. She would serve macaroni and cheese for a few nights afterward, until she could chew solid food again—her way of saying she was sorry for the way things were. Afterward, he would hear his mother and her boyfriend in the bedroom next to his. In his life, he has heard more passion than he has tasted.

His mother showed him it was a woman's job to anticipate. It had not occurred to him that a shy and soft-mannered woman might take offense to his ways. He had never struck his wife. That should count for something. But instead of feeling grateful, Juanita seemed to resent him. He could not put his finger on the problem. A man who did not strike his wife and still did not get laid was not a man.

The crazy business of a woman—that she could change so much! His wife was as willing and compliant as any of Lázaro's women when they first met. Not as beautiful, short, and shy—still fresh from the ways of her tribe, she moved with the sinewy grace of a jaguar. But the years brought change. Now she walked with purpose. Purpose. More than anything else, he resents this about her. A man needs passion. When a woman pours water on her fire, there is only smoke to remind of the heat that was lost.

He knows what Lázaro is thinking: *let each man work his clay in his own way*. He has seen the women who come to the pottery shops in Mata Ortiz. They sizzle with heat that burns a man's insides. It is hard to visit Lázaro and to watch the women captivate with their eyes. Easier to pretend that the women tease him as well. Lázaro does not deserve anger. He is a good man, a generous man who would share his women if he knew of Esquivel's ache. But hunger for a woman is not a thing he can confide, even if the others are willing tonight. If a man cannot coax desire from his own wife, he should hide the fact. Let his wife tell her friends if she will. A man should not brag of his failures.

His friend basks in the admiration his words have earned. Lázaro is a skilled man who has taught himself to combine beauty with function. He deserves what he has created. In the cantina tonight, he doesn't take more than his share. Perhaps Lázaro does not think less of a friend whose wife looks through him as though he doesn't exist. Maybe Lázaro would understand it is a woman's way of showing she is immune—her way of thinking. Nothing he has done.

Still, the thought persists; *maybe he, Esquivel Martinez, deserves the life he has created, as well.*

Esquivel moves to the fire. In the crest of glistening logs, he imagines a woman's triangle nesting. He watches transfixed as the flame devours the mirage, melding it with the fire's heat. For the instant he feels the Greek girl against him, imagines the taste, the scent of olive oil on his tongue. He turns and finds a seat to hide his trembling.

Lázaro is speaking again, his mood lethargic as though he has been hypnotized by his own words. For now, his tongue has taken over for his judgment. Tomorrow he will remember and will be too ashamed to drink beside his friends. Tonight, Esquivel is embarrassed for him, but there is nothing he can do.

————

"I LIGHT THE CANDLES, and the light whispers. Her skin drinks from the room. Brown skin is very beautiful in the candlelight, no?" The Mexicans nod, all except Mendoza. The gringos nod, also, even the blonde man who thinks his is the only way. The *americano* seems riveted to the words. Lázaro opens his palm to reveal two stones worn smooth from use.

"These are the small stones I use to polish the clay. The same I use to polish the woman's skin. Rub her. Feel her heat. Sometimes, I use the animal bones the ancients showed us to use on the pots, just to test her. To see if she will protest. But my women, they know me. Never would I risk this trust. Everything a man does, it should be for pleasure."

The others hesitate. Some seem about to object, but what can they say? Only Mendoza moves, shifting with a raw, primitive growl—the sound a jackal makes. "You are a man-whore! You want your women to carve their names on the post outside your door!" He drains his glass and glares at Esquivel for another. Lázaro tilts back on his bench and makes as if to rise.

Esquivel shakes his head in warning. There is more than impatience on Mendoza's part. He carries a knife for reasons that most men would not. There are rumors about him in the village—where his house sits alone, away from the others—about sharp cries and beatings in the night. Esquivel tries to take the thought from his mind. Casa Corte is a small village. Sometimes, such matters are best left undisturbed, like the carrion of the dead animals left for the buzzard.

He recalls the rumor that Mendoza keeps a chain beside his bed, one end attached to the metal bed frame. Of what use are such thoughts? It is the nature of his village that Conchita's beating at the hands of Mendoza incited the men to fury. A whore belongs to all. When one of the men takes liberties with a common woman, the others suffer. But a wife is a different matter. Who is to care that she doesn't emerge from the house, doesn't appear on market day? It is no one's concern unless she gives testimony to *la policía,* and what woman would do that to her husband?

Lázaro heeds the warning. He sits back as though to say he will tolerate interruption, but not by Mendoza. "I use the tip of her hair like a brush, painting her body with bath water—or sometimes the wine from my glass— stroking while our blood warms. When her hair tickles, she laughs. I like a woman with laughter in her throat. You know? A woman who laughs leaves her anger at the door."

Esquivel remembers a time before laughter disappeared from his bedroom. Laughter is the thing that a man misses in the later years. A woman's breasts can go soft. It is sourness a man hates. Esquivel recalls one of his neighbors who drinks in the cantina sometimes but returns home to spend his evenings with his wife. One day, he watched his neighbor slap his woman on her rump, a teasing swat that brought a saucy reaction—even in the public street.

The memory of the wife's reaction played in his mind for many days, the quick, smiling response as she tossed her head and pretended to be outraged. Later, he tried the same slap on Juanita's rump, but her fury caused her to spill the pottery tray of steaming frijoles she carried. It was only a tap. A mistake. It would not happen again. The next time he saw the neighbor, he turned away and pretended to clean the battery connector of his Chevrolet Impala until the couple passed. When the man comes into the cantina, Esquivel tries to put the picture from his mind. But it is hard, sometimes.

Lázaro is drunk, or he would not be telling so much about himself. Never has Esquivel heard him speak of these things. Perhaps it is fate that brings up the words tonight. For whatever reason, it is good to hear so much. When he is sober, his friend saves his honesty for the clay.

"A woman likes to feel warmth. I kneel at her feet and pour *agua* from a pitcher. I watch her release. Trusting. I bring the temperature of the water to that of her body, so there is no telling where one begins and the other ends. Under my hands, she relaxes. When a woman trusts, her body releases its passion."

Esquivel considers the dark-haired gringo, the one with the bold young wife. It is good that he listens. His wife has a playful nature—maybe she will not turn sour. Juanita was a child when he found her. A child still, two years later, when he pulled aside her nightdress on their wedding night while she watched with dark-eyed trust. When he found her passage so tight he thought it would tear, he took his time. Although he never told her of them, his wife should be glad of the girls he had loved before her, because they prepared him to be more than the rutting bulls his mother had found.

The first few times, he found his wife watching him, trusting him to know. He focused on her, and for a while, he was almost glad that she was not the Greek girl. But before long, his memories began to betray him. It was not enough that his wife allowed him. Even though her moans made him burst with pride, he wanted the passion of the girl on the beach, her playfulness. Each morning, he woke before the roosters and stretched his muscles, hoping to find them sore with satisfaction and hard use. But it was not to be.

This is the feeling he misses. His wife is not playful.

Lázaro continues. "There is no hurry. With my pots, I want to be proud of what I have created. Love is no different. A woman properly loved will carry the memory always."

The *americano* nods. He remains silent in order to preserve the mood, but his face reveals his understanding. He is a man who remembers.

Mendoza snorts, a sound not lost on the others. He grips his glass, his fingers cracked from chemicals or the sun, his fingernails chipped and broken. His forearms are crisscrossed with angry, jagged welts from his fighting roosters.

Esquivel shudders, thinking of the fate of any fighting

cock that would open the skin of Jose Mendoza. He turns away, half wishing he possessed such nerve.

Mendoza speaks to Lázaro Quezada as if to a cur dog. "You are a fool, amigo. What kind of man gives his pleasure to the woman? You take what you want. Women know this. They expect it."

The hatred of many years fills Lázaro Quezada. He knows of the abuse that Mendoza gives his wife. He has seen the way the shy daughter watches him with her dark eyes, how she hides the crippled leg that her father caused her. Village gossip is not always accurate. He and Esquivel have spoken of the rumor, but it re-ignites in his mind. The priest knows the truth of the matter. Mendoza has earned his reputation. He deserves what he gets. Someone should take the knife he uses to threaten the weaker men and turn it on him. Then his daughter would be free.

Lázaro has drunk too much tonight. He should find a better time to take his anger out on Mendoza, when his head is clear. Tonight, his reactions are as slow as a hibernating rattlesnake. He must keep his anger in check.

The others lean close to hear his soft rebuke. "Watch the butterflies when they hatch, Mendoza. When they let go of their fear they fly. Maybe that's what you are afraid of! You only take a woman who is too frightened to move?"

Mendoza rises half to his feet, his eyes the color of flint, narrow and fury-filled. "You sack of *mierda!*" he bellows.

Esquivel finds his voice over the thickening of fear. "Let it alone, Mendoza. Sit down. Finish your drink." His chuckle feels hollow. "No sense in wasting good cerveza, huh, amigo?" He waits until Mendoza slumps back.

The priest has been waiting. Now he speaks. "Señor Mendoza...you are a cruel man."

The eyes darken. Mendoza makes a small movement with his hand under the table. "And you have a wish to die."

The priest is undeterred. "The women say your wife carries the brand of your cattle burned on her flesh. Is this so?"

Mendoza laughs. "Maybe you want to lift her skirts and see for yourself?"

The priest's face blazes, but he says nothing. He lowers his eyes to the table and pretends he does not grasp the significance of the insult.

The blonde gringo is quick to comprehend. "You insult a man of God! Maybe someone ought to kill you, bastard!"

Mendoza laughs again, pleased at their reaction. "Maybe you will think to try, *perrito*?"

"Someone ought to gut you with that knife and leave you for the coyotes. Serve you right. Damned pervert!"

The idea is amusing. Mendoza tears open his shirt, bares his chest, then reaches for his knife and parts the air with its blade. He rams it point-down into the table. "Here...I give you first pass. Go ahead. *Dame la chota!* Give me the cigarette butt. Fight me!"

The cowboy Josh half crouches, and his arm streaks for the handle. Before he can grab it, his friend cuffs his wrist and twists him sideways, smashing his face into the tabletop. The whoosh of air through his compressed lips is the only sound except the swish of the overhead fan.

Mendoza wipes drool with his bandanna. "Maybe you are smarter than you look, *perrito*."

The little cowboy glares hatred over his shoulder as his friend drags him to the door and slams it behind them.

For a moment, the room is quiet. From outside, the blonde cowboy lets off a high-pitched scream of rage.

Then there is the sound of a truck door slamming as though the two intend to drive off into the night. But their money is still on the table. The dark-haired cowboy returns alone.

Esquivel forces his laugh. "Go on with your story, Lázaro. Maybe we make ourselves a clay woman before we leave tonight, huh?"

"Nah. The mood is for shit."

The others shift on their benches. The priest makes his way to the door leading outside. A minute later he returns, and the *americano* rises and follows to empty his bladder as well.

Mendoza is not ready for the attention to pass from him so soon. He turns to the dark-haired American. "Hey, Jeem...the potter talks like a *joto*. Like your pretty friend out there. Pain is what a man uses! A woman who fears you, she will not bother to think! Use her hard. The same as with a dog. Or a horse."

The cowboy Josh is outside. His friend Jim does not rise to the challenge. Mendoza's goad is wasted.

The others have heard enough. "Shut up. Let the potter finish," the guitar player says. Even he is tired of Mendoza.

Esquivel glances to see whether Lázaro has taken offense. His friend has avoided drinking with Mendoza for a lot of years—until tonight. It remains to be seen if he will walk out and let the slamming door finish his story. The cowboy Josh has returned. Esquivel nods to encourage Lázaro. There will be another time to deal with Mendoza; the *javelina* is too drunk to know the difference between good conversation and noise.

For Lázaro, the mood is ruined. "Nothing more to say. That is what I know about women. That they come to me. And that they say I am a good dancer..." His words coast to a halt. He cannot concentrate on romance when violence fills the air. Like smoke from the slash-and-burn fires in the jungle, the mood is cut, *corte*.

Mendoza stumbles to the door without bothering to shut it behind him. Esquivel hears his stream of piss hitting the wall outside.

CHAPTER FOURTEEN

Corte: As the cut of the river

The heat in Casa Corte is dry, not heavy and thick like in the jungle near Yucatan or at the coast near Acapulco. The heat in Casa Corte is quick and thin, *corte*, dry as the bleached bones of animals caught between the *bochorno*, water holes—unfriendly heat in a land where caution has its place.

Before Mendoza can stumble back into the room, The cowboy Josh begins to talk. Esquivel turns his attention to the cowboy. He will have the best story, one about the hunger of desire. He wears his passion like cologne, so it enters the room before him.

"I got enough trouble for two men," he says. "Dad wants me to move on home, take over. I do the best I can, but it's never enough. I sneak off now and again. Do a little rodeoing. Spent last summer with my sister in Seattle. She got me a job with some sports catalog. Posing for pictures. Whole lot easier than herding cattle. Course that's not how the folks see it. My old man wants me to take over the ranch so bad he can taste it. Works my ass off."

His friend had heard the story before. "Ah, come on, Josh. He's not that bad. Least you got an old man."

"I ain't so sure about that."

"You're his hope." Jim is making an argument for his own sons, should it ever come to that.

The blonde cowboy pulls a crumpled pack of Marlboros from his rolled-up sleeve and taps a cigarette into his left hand. He searches his pocket for his lighter, lights up, and draws before he answers. "Then he's in a tight bind. I ain't hope enough for no one. I don't want that ranch and he knows it. Not on his terms."

"What terms? Marry, settle down, take over? Don't sound that bad."

"I'm tired of him making my decisions. I ain't him!"

"What's going on, Josh? You got beans where your brains used to be?"

"Maybe." His cigarette is a stall for time. New smoke swirls through the late-night anger.

"*Maybe* nothing! Something's bugging you."

"Maybe it's none of your business."

"Got something to do with that gal you're seeing? Hear she's in a hurry to get married. Why not? Marriage would settle you. Keep you from chasing yourself into a spin. It's time, you know."

"Time to get married and throw a few calves? You sound like my old man."

"Maybe he's right."

"Maybe you're a liar!"

"Maybe you're drunk. You always drink too much. Another couple of years, you won't be any good to your old man or the rodeo. You're killing yourself, you know that?"

"Family tradition. We race to see who can pickle our liver first. Why you care? You got what you wanted. I got nothing but a pair of empty pockets."

"Marry that gal. I heard you two arguing. She's ready and you're not. Same old story. She'll leave you. Next time you see her, she'll be married to some cowboy, with a bun in the oven. That what you want?"

"Maybe."

"Jeesh."

Esquivel listens to the exchange. For Jim, the choice was easy, but Esquivel has more sympathy. If the girl is not the right one, nothing makes sense. Maybe the man is in love with his friend's wife. Maybe his friend does not know this; he does not seem to be a man who thinks much beyond what is said.

Jim's friend Josh does not think too much, either. He is afraid of what he might uncover. Better for him, the *cerveza*, the drunkenness. He has made a friend of his drunkenness. His mannerisms are those of habit—the exaggeration of his movements, the care he takes to set his glass down carefully on the table so as not to draw attention.

Mendoza watches. Esquivel sees the glazed hunger in Mendoza's face, and he tries to tear his gaze away, unsure what he is seeing. But Mendoza's actions do not lie. His heavy lids are partially closed, but they don't mask his agony. His lips part with an inaudible moan, and he shifts to readjust himself.

The flare in his eyes is gone so quickly that Esquivel might have missed it, but he recalls a story one of the miners told one night when Mendoza was not in the cantina. A handful of Indians sat alone, talking now and then, making their drinks last. The talk that night was of Mendoza and the small boy he used for his pleasure in the mine, when the others were too busy to notice. Each of the miners, made brave by their *pulque*, thought they would have stopped him had they known, but the truth is, maybe, maybe not.

The boy told no one. For many months he kept his secret until he was feverish with pain and could no longer piss. When herbs did not work, the boy was carried to the doctor, who explained in a gentle voice that gonorrhea was a disease that could be cured only when small boys gave up their secrets. After many minutes, the boy's shaking voice whispered, "Mendoza."

Mendoza went back to work at the mine, vowing revenge. The boy found a benefactor who paid his way to the mission school run by the Sisters of Natividad.

Tonight Mendoza watches the blonde cowboy with enough heat that it could ignite the fresh cigarette dangling from the gringo's lips. When the cowboy turns, Mendoza's eyes blaze with contempt. The others don't see the desire, only hear his words as they cut the room. His loathing is loud, filled with obscenities. "*Joto!* Hey, *Maricóne*, you make me puke."

The blonde cowboy's laugh is shaky. He turns to his friend. "You want to know my first love? Drove me crazy I wanted it so bad."

"What was that?"

He recovers his force. "That old yellow GMC pickup your dad bought off the salvage yard. Remember when we were fifteen? Driving to school? Man, I loved that pickup!"

"Yeh. It was twenty years old and looked fifty. Came in second best, time I ran it into a fence post. Remember?"

"You jumped out and booted in the door, you were so crazy mad. Man, those were good times." Josh laughs at the memory.

His friend joins him. "Kept an old *Hustler* magazine under the seat."

"Man, Jim, I loved that bench seat—felt like leather, even if it wasn't. I remember wiping it down with Lexol. Polishing it with your old tee shirt. Before the prom."

"Right before you cut that six-inch gash in the Naugahyde with the hoof pick in your pocket. Tore right through. After that, couldn't keep the kapok in. The springs pinched my balls every time we hit a bump. I finally threw an old horse blanket on it to keep from losing something I figured I'd need." Jim's laughter shows he has forgiven his friend.

When the blonde begins again, his tone is lazy, reminiscent, the easy griping of someone who has no complaint with the past. "Sheesh! Wipers never worked. We drove blind every time it rained. I'd stick my head out the window and watch for the turnoff."

"Never rained at our place, anyway. Summer hit, I forgot how bad those wipers were. By the time the rains came again, I always had something better to do with my money."

"Heater had one setting—*On*. And no defroster. Remember when we knocked that plug of Copenhagen inside the vent and couldn't get it fished out?"

"Truck sounds like a sack of shit to me." Mendoza wants the room's attention.

Jim ignores him. No one else in the room had a truck when they were fifteen or they would say so. "Wasn't just the truck, was it, Josh?"

"Hell, no. I loved riding home from a movie on the nights when we didn't have dates. Watching you spin that brodie knob on your steering wheel. You could spin that wheel faster'n anybody I ever saw. We did brodies in the sand, down by the riverbed. Sand flying up. Your elbow hung out the window while you was doing easy donuts. Used to watch you out of the corner of my eye. Figured if we wrecked, they would probably leave what was left of us in the truck and bury us that way."

"Heck, Josh. It ain't like we were married!"

Josh feels the silence. The room is waiting. He punches his friend on the arm and picks up his hat. "Come on. Let's go see if the flood's rising."

He's outside before his friend has a chance to set his glass down.

Neither man is in any shape to drive, but it is none of Esquivel's business. In the distance, the river still roars. He does not warn them about the channels that will cave under their tires if they get too close. The two will take their chances. He and the others remain at their seats while the night fills with the sounds of a gunning engine and the yelps of drunken men at play.

———

FOR FIFTEEN MINUTES, they spin circles in the sand, their headlights gleaming through the window with each pass. When the game is finished, the two return, laughing like children. Their breath comes in gasps, but they are relaxed. More to the point, they have brought fresh energy inside with them.

Their flushed faces recall for Esquivel a time when his mother paid for him to travel with a church group to the Sierra Nevada to play in the snow. He remembers the feel of the cold on his feet because he did not own a pair of boots or enough socks or dry jeans to change at the end of the day. The trip is not one that fits well in his memory. But for these cowboys, playfulness is part of their nature. He smiles despite himself. It is hard to dislike men who are good-natured in their drinking. "So which won out, the old pickup or the truck you drive today?" he asks.

The blonde cowboy answers first. "Nothing's as good as I remember."

"Heck, Josh, that's because you don't let go of anything. You're still mad at your old man for the way he taught you to ride."

Josh turns to make his case to Esquivel. "My old man takes me out and decides to teach me everything I need to know about cattle in one day. He shouts, 'Ride pell-mell for the fence, then pull up your horse up, hard.' 'Why?' I asked him. 'What's the point?' It didn't make sense."

"He wanted you to—" his friend interrupts.

"I know, now. But I was a kid. 'Stead of explaining, he told me, 'Get out of here. Go on up to the house.' He gave me one day to learn. Then he gave up like I was too stupid. That's why I spent so much time at your place. Learning off your dad."

"Mom cooked enough meals for you. She joked you'd moved in."

"Wanted to."

"She'd a let you, Josh."

"Should have. Never saw your mother take a drink."

"Yeah. I guess your mom…everybody knew she liked to party."

"Party!" The word sounded vulgar. Even the priest looked up, surprised at the anger in Josh's tone.

Jim isn't as forgiving. His voice is tight. "What'd your mother do that you're not doing now? You been drinking as long as I've known you."

"You don't see me trying to rear a couple of kids."

Jim made a quick swipe across his lip with a finger. "Your loss. Closest I ever felt to God was the first time my wife took our baby to her breast. Something about the way she looked at him. Made me feel like the odd man out. But I know what I felt."

The *americano* follows the conversation without joining in. If Esquivel were a betting man, he would say that the old gringo has no children. Either that or they have chosen to live without his influence, one the same as the other. He shifts, not meaning to, but stillness has caught in his muscle.

The cowboy Jim looks up and notices that others are listening. In the movement, the mood is broken.

Josh has one last thought. "I had a kid like that once. My girlfriend's little boy, about four. He followed me around all day, asking questions. 'Why don't carrots grow sideways? Why don't the dog and the cat get married?' Why, why, why? I didn't have much going on with his mom, but I stayed a lot longer than I meant to. Didn't want to give him up."

Esquivel watches. Josh has seen God in a child. He is not as lost as he seems.

His friend Jim intervenes. "Get yourself to church. Trust me on this. Marry her."

Anger flares. There are still disagreements between friends. "You church people always got the answers." Josh's anger speaks for Esquivel as well. "Hell, maybe I should go to the priest's church over here. He looks like he's got as many answers as the rest of us."

The priest rouses, considers his response, and looks down at his glass. When he speaks, his voice is hoarse. "You're feeding the wrong dog."

Josh wants to argue, but he does not know how to respond to the priest's quiet certainty, so he asks, "What dog?"

The priest has waited for such a moment. He shifts on his bench. "When I was a young priest, an old man came up to me after Mass one Sunday. I had seen him in church that day, but he didn't seem to care much for what I was saying. 'Padre,' he said to me, 'You and me, we are alike.

See, I got two dogs, live inside me. One is a barking dog. A big, mean dog. He barks and growls, and he gives me no rest. Sometimes I want to lie down, but he won't let me. I never know when this dog will make trouble. Angry and bullying, fighting until sometimes I can't hear the sound of my own thoughts.'

"And he said, 'I have another dog inside me. It is a quiet dog, a napping dog. In the afternoons, he wants to sleep beside me in the shade. At night, he comes, and I rub his ears. When I am sad, this dog comes to lick my hand. He never tries to take what doesn't belong to him. Never fights over the bone I give to the other. I like both my dogs, but sometimes I need to choose, and it's hard.' 'Which one do you need?' I asked. 'I need both,' he answered. 'Then which of your two dogs is bigger?' I asked, because this would tell me much. 'The one I feed the most,' he said. 'The one I feed the most.'"

In the room, no one moves. For a minute, maybe ninety seconds, the room is quiet while the men consider the priest's words. It is these moments Esquivel savors, when his cantina and the men are *simpáticos*.

Even Mendoza is affected. He rouses and slurs, "You're feeding the wrong dog."

CHAPTER FIFTEEN

Cortarse: To be embarrassed, shy

T he young *indio* listens intently to the gringo cowboys' conversation. He knows some English, but not enough to follow the argument —only the anger. He hides his interest and sips occasionally on his *cerveza*. When he grows weary of sitting, he rises to scan the bus schedule on the wall, returns to his seat, and glances out the window at the darkness, in a hurry to be somewhere else. Esquivel watched him all night, and the boy has not spoken.

Esquivel is only half right. The Indian guitar player, Taxco Verones, drinks sparingly because he finds the stories intoxicating. To add *cerveza* would muddle his brain beyond reason. He watches the gringos and tries to imagine how it would feel to be so sure of himself. The others, he has little use for. He does not need a priest, and he will find his own way with his woman, not the potter's way. His stopping at *Esquivel's* is a quirk of fate.

He studies the olive limbs burning in the fireplace and wishes he could travel like the smoke.

The sky in Casa Corte is cleaner, broader, wider than he remembers. In Los Angeles, it was barely noticeable, hidden for days under a layer of brown smog. Even the mountains, only thirty miles distant, hidden.

In Los Angeles, he killed pigs, the same as in Petatlán. The money was good in California—better than he earned in Mexico. Even if the work was the same. In Petatlán, he took turns hitting hogs on the head, then hanging them on hooks by their hocks and slitting their necks with sticking knives until they bled into tubs set on the steaming sand. After they were gutted, he helped dunk their bodies into vats of boiling water drawn from the Rio San Jeronimito by the women who wash their clothes in the thin river. Before they cooled, he scraped the bristles from the hide. Afterward, he tossed the butchered carcasses into an old, windowless Volkswagen bus for delivery to the *carnicerías*, the meat markets and the *restaurantes*.

The smell of the slaughterhouse was bad, tallow and entrails. But it is the terror of the trapped hogs that drives his nightmares, crying sounds such as a child would make. He made up his mind to leave Petatlán one scorching afternoon while riding in the back of an old van with his knees on the stiff carcasses so they wouldn't roll. He fought flies and stench while the van lurched through the traffic. On a sharp corner, his knee buckled, and he slipped. For the fifteen seconds it took to pull himself off the smooth, sticky corpses, he lay suffocated by the pile of squealing children he had killed. The sound revisits him in his dream. This is why he left his home and traveled north.

He is proud to be Zapoteca, descended from the people of the Costa Grandes who claimed the land long before Cortés or even Friar de Garrovillas. But the people in Los Angeles do not care about such things. To them, he was only a Mexican. In Los Angeles, he did not get a job he wanted because the hiring boss said he would be lazy. But the man is wrong. A man is not lazy because he understands to live in harmony with the seasons.

His escape from Petatlán turned out to be a matter of degree. He wanted a job at a restaurant, washing dishes or bussing tables. But the slaughterhouse boss was not particular about a green card, and he was able to catch a ride to work. In the end, practical matters settled his mind. In Los Angeles, a noisy ventilation system removed some of the stench, but killing pigs was grisly work in Petatlán, and no better there. On his first day, he stood outside the slaughterhouse and prepared himself for the squealing.

After the first year, it was in his mind to quit, slip back over the border, and catch a ride home for Christmas, but he was not sure he would be able to return. Some of his roommates, the ones with legal green cards, returned south for the Christmas celebrations and weddings of their friends. By the second year, he had saved his money. When December came again, he took his earnings and headed home.

Sometimes the memory comes back in strange moments, like today on the bus from Ciudad Juárez. As the bus traveled the straight ribbon of desert highway for six hours, he tried to block out the tedium of the passing sand and cacti. He saw a half-dozen boxcars where small children played among the weeds and broken siding. At some point, he managed to fall asleep—until his nightmare jarred him awake. In his dream, he was clubbing and sticking endless, squealing pigs. He awoke in a rush, his stomach heaving. When the bus stopped for passengers in Casa Corte, he made his way to the roadway.

When the bus left, minutes later, he was still emptying his stomach behind a scrub cactus.

In the cantina, he is surprised that the gringos care so much about what their women think of them. He would not be as open. He might learn from a whore, but he will not tell his woman. It will be none of her business. These men have known many women. He has known none yet, except to watch the ones that visited the house in Los Angeles to service the men on payday. But he will not share his story with these men. They would only laugh— either in his face or behind it, which would be worse. His stories are in his head.

He starts at the beginning.

IN ZIHUATANEJO, smoke ripens the air with smells of rotting plants and burning hillsides. When the *cocos* fall to the ground, their tough fiber shells protect them from exploding in the heat. Although he is only fourteen, Taxco feels like he is one of them, a *coco*, he has scaled so many trunks with his bare feet. Every day, he collects them in a woven basket strapped across his back. Taking time to drink from his bottle and to eat what his mother has prepared. *Cocos* fall all the months of the year. He will have this occupation for as long as his nerve will allow. He does not plan to fall like his father did. Crippled or not, Alberto Verones is still master of his house. He takes the money Taxco earns, proud that his son is not weak like his mother, cringing and crying.

Most days, Taxco manages to hide a few *centavos*, folded in a paper sleeve and taped to the bottom of his drawer, before his father demands his earnings. His father is too crippled to creep on his knees and search.

One afternoon, he ventures into the market for a cone

of vanilla *helados* at the tiny stall his friend tends in an alley off the Avenida de Cinco de Mayo. In the unlit stall, he sees her, a young girl sitting still and watchful in the stifling heat while the cruise ship tourists make their selections. He is glad she does not hawk her wares like some of the others. She watches without saying anything, and he knows with his first glance that he loves her.

She is new to the shop, new to Zihua—he would know her otherwise. She is young. He guesses ten years old because her breasts have not begun to mound beneath the strip of polyester she wears. At first, he thinks she does not study him the way that he studies her, but he is wrong. He looks up, and she averts her eyes.

The brick floor steams with the water she has thrown down to cool the sunbaked bricks. A small fan buzzes nearby. It whips the loose strands of hair escaped from her braid. She sits without complaint, but he is angry that she must suffer. The sheen on her face reminds him of sugar glaze and he is struck with the desire to kiss her cheek. It is midday, and the owner will not return for two hours. Another vendor dozes in the empty shop. Taxco wants to show the girl how he can climb to the top of the *coco* tree to catch the breeze from the *Bahia de Zihuatanejo*, the bay. Instead, he pretends to study the hammocks that she sells. Finally, he asks, "You work alone?"

"My aunt is sick."

"What's your name?"

"Elena."

It is too bad about her aunt. He hopes Elena has a secret place where she hides her earnings. His decision is quick. He tries to make his voice sound deeper, decisive, like the older boys who hang out at the billiard room over the *mercado*. "Amigo...watch this stall for a while, heh?" The boy in the next alcove nods sleepily. Taxco turns to

the girl and sees her hesitation. "Follow me. Who will
know?"

She follows him through the streets to a row of
banyan trees and *coco* palms at the water's edge. They
ignore a skinny dog hunting for scraps. Quick as an
iguana, Taxco climbs the tree and throws the *coco* down.
He descends to feel her admiration close at hand.

"You are a good climber."

"It is nothing."

"It is. You swim, too?"

"A little."

He waits while she pulls her skirt between her brown
legs and into her waistband, then follows her into the
soft, rippling water. The girl's eyes shine with joy when
the cool water hits. Taxco is young. He will forget many
things, but he will remember the happiness of the day.

Tonight, when he played his guitar in the cantina, his
fingers recalled this.

When they are cool, they start back. She is from Zacat-
ula, a small village to the north where the Rio Balsas
empties into the sea. Her uncle will send her back if she
does not earn her keep. She likes it here. The heat is
everywhere, but Zihuatanejo is more to her liking. Her
eyes tell Taxco that there is more for her in Zihua than
just the water. Later, she tells him in a quiet manner that
she will be there again tomorrow, and every day after,
until her aunt is well.

CHAPTER SIXTEEN

Corte: To cut, as to insult

Casa Corte is not the place to talk about oneself. Here, a person's business is his own. Sometimes the gringos come to take photographs and to ask questions, but the people here are slow to answer. They have their ways. Their memories are for themselves, like the ancient piece of lace or the tarnished Spanish bridle locked in a leather trunk.

Mendoza pours a *cerveza* down his throat. When he finishes, he wipes his mouth with the back of his hand and crows. A movement recalls the blonde cowboy to Mendoza. "Mind your business, pretty boy. Or I give you some of my own," he growls.

The cowboy's words are slurred. "Hear that, bartender? You've got a dang psycho over here!"

Esquivel waggles his index finger from side to side, but the cowboy does not heed his warning.

Mendoza does not let it lie. "Keep talking that way,

gringo. After I slit your throat, maybe the priest here will say a prayer for you. Hey, amigo?" The priest does not look up. "Hey priest—you got time for a funeral *mañana*?" The priest does not answer. "Hey, *cabrón*, I'm talking to you!"

"Shut your trap." The cowboy Josh is on his feet. The pearl snaps on his cuff catch the firelight. His arm throws a lightning jab that catches Mendoza. The silence clatters, and Mendoza's bench falls to its side. He lunges unsteadily to his feet. The gringo's fist glances off the Mexican's face. He is too drunk to register pain. He swings clumsily, connects, and sends the gringo sprawling. The gringo cowboy rolls to his feet and slams his knee into Mendoza's groin, bending him in half. Mendoza roars and lunges, black eyes flashing hatred, spittle spraying the room.

The cowboy Jim Patterson grabs his friend from behind. Lázaro tries to do the same with Mendoza, but Mendoza is not so easy. The fight is now between the two of them as Mendoza tries to twist from Lázaro's wrist lock. Lázaro locks Mendoza until it seems his arm will snap. Mendoza hesitates, and the fight is lost. Before Lázaro can release him, the cowboy Josh pulls loose and grabs Mendoza's knife from its sheath. Lázaro wavers. If he does not release Mendoza, he will be party to murder.

Jim grabs his friend's wrist and the knife drops to the floor with a metallic clank. "You crazy fool! You want to rot in a Mex jail?"

The room swelters with anger. Esquivel collects the knife, as much for something to do as for any other reason. He glances toward his telephone but remembers the line is dead. *La policía* have enough to do tonight.

"A Mex jail? The *burra* won't live that long!" Mendoza shrugs off Lázaro. His fingers twitch toward the knife still in Esquivel's hand, but he doesn't act on the idea.

Instead, he rights his bench and straddles it. With stiff fingers, he reaches for his crumpled pack of cigarettes and pulls one out.

Esquivel returns to the bar and pours himself a *cerveza*. Mendoza's words are bold, but they do not ring true. Mendoza is a coward. He will not fight a willing man. He picks, instead, on the small men, Tarahumara workers who tolerate insult to keep their jobs.

The priest surprises. "The people are right, Mendoza, when they call you a *javelina*."

"You think so, priest? So now I am a *javelina*? A pig?"

"In Mexico, there is always a reason." The priest does not rise to anger.

Esquivel studies the thin set of Mendoza's lips and thinks that a man must sleep with hate for his muscles to set so tight.

The priest speaks to the table. "The trouble with Mendoza—he has no dream left except to be feared. Such a man is the walking dead!"

Chapter Seventeen

Corte: Cut as one's ties

The night reasserts itself with the rustling of the pepper tree outside the door. In the distance, a coyote cries, a series of whoops answered by another, closer.

Taxco raises his head to listen to the mating calls. How easy it is for the coyote to find a mate, easier than for most men. In Zihuatanejo, an *indio* boy with a crippled father and a weak mother does not go to school, but if he keeps his eyes and ears open, he learns many things.

Taxco has a story, better than he has heard tonight, but he does not share it. The memory makes him anxious. It seems more than a year ago, the night when he climbed up the arroyo in Central California. From the village, it looked easier. By his third step, he was crouching like a cat, wedging his toe into the baked adobe earth. A hundred feet ahead lay the base of a plain block letter S. The lady at *la abacería*, the market, told him some local boys dug it out of the hillside long ago and filled it with cement. He could barely make out the words *twenty-five years ago* from the rapid stream of English she spewed while she wrapped his tripe in a square sheet of butcher paper.

Twenty-five years earlier, the *gringo* boys graduated from high school and left to take office jobs in the cities. This last part he guesses at because there are no young white men left, only old men and women, laborers like himself, and poor families who buy cheap houses.

They stand outside and water their weedy lawns and the orange flowers that grow along their fences. He likes the plants that grow on the hillsides around his village—the plants his friends call *la pochota, el bocote, el cirlán*. He doesn't have English names for them. Only for Mexican cactus. His kind of grass grows on the hillsides: wild oats and foxtail dried to golden blonde that cause his cowboy boots to slide when he climbs.

That afternoon, he started to climb. Once, twice, he slipped, but it felt good to challenge the gringo hill. Ten steps farther, he made it to the first of the cement strips, this one the foot of the *S*, not curved like a woman, but at right angles, plain and square. As though whoever built it did not want to stay too long on the hillside. Up close, it was cruder than he expected, rough, with scraps of lumber splintered in the sand. He gave the rotten form a kick and watched as it tore loose and slid down the slope.

He noticed the hillside the first day he rode into the valley. Wondered why the gringos would whitewash a letter on the side of a hill. The town was named Shandon. Maybe the *S* was put there to demonstrate the villagers' love for their valley. If that were the case, he spit at their devotion. A thing of pride belonged higher, near the top so the villagers could see it from a great distance. Instead, it looked pitiful, resting barely above the swell of the rounded hill that he named *la chicha*. If the hill were really a woman's breast, this *S* would be lost underneath her fullness, not even nipple high.

He faced the town and blew from his nostrils to show his disdain. In Mexico, women take pride in the symbols of their village. The entire community turns out, the men to whitewash the church walls, the women to scrub pews and windows while the children bring flowers for the altar.

His anger threw him off balance. He twisted to keep from falling forward and landed heavily on the cement. When his heart settled, he surveyed what he could see of the valley. Before him, the setting sun shaded the riverbed. Rays of light played on the top of the sycamores and willows while their branches sheltered dozing cattle. *La abacera*, the grocer lady, told him, while she weighed his pinto beans, that this river joined another, an upside-down river eighteen miles to the west. *Norte*, she told him proudly. "The Salinas runs north."

In the cantina, he pulls a crumpled pack of Marlboros from his pocket and lights one. Just as he did that night on the hill.

A *lagartija* scurried across the cement, and he followed the lizard's path with the glowing tip of his cigarette. When it neared the edge, he gave the cigarette a quick jab. The lizard whipped its tail from side to side and disappeared over the edge. Scrawnier than the geckos of Zihuatanejo, this one was nothing. He took a satisfied drag on his cigarette. This night, he was *la migra*, and the lizard was the prey. "Hide, little *lagartija*. Hide. Don't forget to write!" His laughter felt clean in his throat.

In the cantina, he smiles again at the memory. But he will tell no one. Working in the north could have made him a drinker like it did many of his friends. The *cerveza* coaxes thoughts of the girl. Maybe he is weak and uses it as an excuse, but tonight, alcohol satisfies him. The others will get drunk and talk their mouths off. If he were like these men, he could talk about his woman. It would be easier.

In Shandon, he reached inside his shirt and pulled the bottle of *mezcal* from under his arm, unscrewed the cap, and lobbed it into a tumbleweed caught on the highway fence. Five strands of barbed wire kept cattle from straying onto the roadway. At the Rio Grande, the barbed wire tried to keep the wetbacks out. Waste of money. With its lid lost in the weeds, he had no choice but to drain the bottle. The tequila, hot as fire, reamed his throat like that day in the desert when he made the crossing.

A powder blue van roared past, its diesel engine louder than the passenger cars that followed in a tight pack, their drivers frustrated by the lack of passing lanes on this road the natives named Blood Alley. In his mind, the van carried Mexican workers hiding beneath boxes of lettuce. The way he entered the United States on his first visit. It was simple back then. Hitch a ride. No one questioned what was in the truck. And lettuce was good for hiding. *Mexicano* lettuce pickers were welcome in the north until they started sending their children to schools and their pregnant wives to hospitals. When the women's water sacs broke on the shiny tile of the hospital lobbies, border fences went up like the five-strand barbed wire along Blood Alley.

"Too bad, amigo. You must wait your turn. The *coyotes* won't stop their truck for hours yet." He saluted the blue van and watched it dip from sight. The *mezcal* was smooth. It didn't burn like the day the desert robbed him of the mucous inside his mouth and made his tongue swell until he could barely sip the brown, murky water at the cattle pond. He tried, but his throat wouldn't swallow the putrid water.

In the cantina, his memories overlap. The day in Shandon merges with his last border crossing a year earlier. That crossing was hard. Nothing went the way the *coyote* promised. He wandered in the searing heat for two days, half-crazed, praying to be found. It was the smugglers who found him, still alive. He knew then that his mother's prayers had worked.

In Esquivel's, Taxco closes his eyes, swallows another sip of *cerveza*, and waits to see if he will vomit from the bile that rises in his throat.

In the desert, he rose from a pond, wet from the brackish water. His body not cool, but no longer on fire. A dead, bloated pig lay nearby in the sand. He heard a chomping coming from it that sounded like a thousand cropping sheep. But there were no sheep, no meadow. He knew the sound, knew what he had to do. His *tio*, his mother's brother, had told stories of the Apache who lived in the mountains, how they survived raids into the desert.

"Moisture," *Tio* once explained, "Comes from many sources."

He tried to use his *coco* machete like a dinner knife loaded with peas, but he grew impatient when he caught the acrid stench of rotting flesh. He reached into the cavity and felt the squirming maggots, thousands of them writhing on top of each other. He closed his fingers and opened his mouth wide, as wide as he could. Even so, some of the fat white grubs dropped to the dirt. Again and again, he filled his mouth, tossing them like peanuts, chewing to release the moisture. They went down easy—like they were grateful to escape the heat.

Ten steps into the mesquite, the first pain ripped through his belly. He knew to expect it. *Try to keep your liquid down*, he had been told. *You'll die if you puke your moisture into the sand.* He tried, but it was no good. Some of his moisture wiggled on the sand.

"*Puta,*" he had growled.

He looks up to see the priest watching him. For a moment, he thinks he has spoken. *Cristos!* Some of the others who crossed earlier told of killing a rattlesnake with their machetes as it coiled to strike. Stripping the flesh with their teeth while it still writhed. He preferred maggots. Snakes are of the devil.

From the Shandon hillside, he watched a produce truck from the Salinas Valley rumble past. He couldn't read the words, but he recognized the symbol on the side of the truck and the crates, stacked five high on the flatbed trailer. Gringos were *loco* for lettuce. He eats it, but it doesn't fill his stomach or set his brain on fire, and he has little use for anything that doesn't do one or the other.

In Salinas, some of the other men used to piss on the produce when the crew boss wasn't looking. But he has too much respect for the food. In Mexico, the men who work the fields are farmers. It is not until they come north that they become pickers—when the gringos give them that name. It is no one's fault, the way the politics of the field are played. He is a farmer—that is all.

He remembers standing, weaving slightly as he staggered to inspect the outline. *Un ess por la escuela,* an *S* for Shandon High. He is part Shandon, part Zihuatanejo, but he no longer belongs in either place. A poor man is no more than what he does for a living. In the old days, he was a *coco* cutter; everyone knew him as that. Now he picks Cabernet and Sauvignon grapes. He is a farmer. The grapes he planted as bare rootstock grow on the hillsides, inside white PVC pipe-like rolling fields of grave markers. The second year, he returned with a crew to tie the foliage onto wires. By the time they returned to pick the fields, the vines looked more like shaggy scarecrows holding hands across the field. Without him, there would be no crop, no economy.

The border *coyote* supplied him with a green card and asked no questions. It was good, the card. He could stand alongside the others and grin when the authorities pulled up in their green government vans. In the harvesting season, the *Patron* was on their side, shouting at *la migra*, pleading for them to allow the crew to finish their job. During harvest, the green cards looked more authentic to the rich growers than the rest of the year.

———

TAXCO DRAINS the last of his *cerveza* and remembers drinking on the hillside while the sun set. He drank *mezcal* that night in Shandon. He remembers the worm sliding down the inside of the bottle until it reached his tongue. He recalls how he swallowed the pickled worm while he grasped the bottle, curved like a spade.

"*Dame la migra.* Our work should count for something. Not just for lettuce." The *mezcal* fogged his brain. He picked up what was left of the bottle and grasped it like a handle while he dug his way up the hill, weaving. Uncertain. He grabbed a clump of sage, found another, and climbed until he could go no higher. With a rock in one hand, the bottle in the other, he lay flat on his belly and stabbed the sunbaked hillside. "I will build the *gringos' ess.* I will do it better than anyone!"

The trembling started while he lay against the cement and felt loneliness bite into his spine. In that moment, he knew. Without a woman, he could die, and no one would ever know—or care. He closed his eyes and sobbed.

He tried to stand, but the bottle slipped off a rock and broke. Angry, reckless, he dug harder, scratching at the soil while the bushes tore at his arms. He felt himself sliding—ten feet, then twenty—before he broke his fall. At the edge of the *S,* he flopped onto his face and lay still. This time, the tears were for himself. Rising onto his elbow, he shook his free fist, angrier than ever in his life. "I am here now!" he raged to the passing cars. "My blood is Zapotecan. But I am here!" Blood dripped from his hand. He pitched the broken bottle and watched it explode onto the hood of an eighteen-wheeler on the highway below. In the near darkness, he heard the semi's air horn blasting down the road.

When silence returned, he heard his breath—as though his lungs were the air brakes on the truck. He remembers feeling pain in his hand. He stood in silence and watched the car lights while the night softened the tires on the pavement. Until it seemed as though there was no sound at all, only lights and motion. One thought intruded. No more barbed wire.

The walk back to the village was long. It was late when he arrived at the tiny house he shared with the others.

In the cantina, he finishes his *cerveza,* his mind is made up. He will return to Shandon. His children will be born there. The thought makes him smile. *We will climb the hill, and I will show them how to build a proud monument. On the top of the chicha, where everyone can see. And every December, I will return to Zihua and bring a gift—a television or a cell phone to my mother. And to my father, if he is still alive.*

The cantina hums with the noises of drunken men. No one speaks, but neither are they silent. To Taxco, the men seem satisfied. They have shared much. How else does a man learn about life without hearing such stories? Twenty-two years have given him more questions than answers. His body is old—older than the gringo cowboys'. Education allows a man to take his time growing old. Uneducated men work for others. They wear their bodies out.

He returns to an evening in his adolescence—late April when the nights were still inclined to be mild. He was busy doing something his grandmother had asked him to do. Sweeping the patio. He remembers as if it were yesterday, standing at the edge of the yard, hidden by a rack of bougainvillea. Something caused him to turn to the bowl of the hill that catches the setting sun in Zihu-atanejo.

The scene was nothing new. He had seen the light ten thousand times before, but this evening, it was as though the pink-tiled *casas* and the long, two-story apartments had each been painted fresh that day. On most days, the street dust and grime lay trapped against the white-washed walls, but on this day, illuminated by the setting sun, they seemed to explode with pride against the *cerra*.

For a minute, maybe two, his body merged with the light while pleasure flooded through him. The roosters sensed it as well. At the same moment, they each began crowing, answering one another until the pueblo was alive with their noise. He remembers the time—seven o'clock in the evening exactly—because the chimes in the bell tower began to ring. *Uno, dos, tres, cuatro, cinco, seis, siete.* He remembers his body in rhythm with the chimes, intensity, pain, and pleasure building until, as suddenly as it began, everything exploded.

He remembers looking up, surprised that the houses were still standing. As he watched, light moved across the mountain, fading until the Mexican cactus on the hilltop took on the color of evening. As though released, the roosters settled down for the night until even they were still.

A sound in the house brought him to his senses. He

brushed his hair back with hands that shook and crept to the dusty patio, surprised at the irritation in his grandmother's voice as she called for him. When the light was at its brightest, he had taken no notice of the traffic, the birds, even his grandmother calling to him from the *casa*.

In the darkness outside *Esquivel's*, Taxco finishes. His body is languid with the softness of the memory. He will share this story with his *novia*, his sweetheart. When they have made love for the first time and she is no longer a virgin, they will talk of quiet things. He will tell her of the sunset. He will tell her how their first time was, for him, like that day. She will recognize it for what it is.

For this reason, he refused the whores who came to service the men on payday in the house in Los Angeles.

CHAPTER EIGHTEEN

Cortar: To become separated, cut off

Esquivel watches the young man fight off sleep. He eyes the tortillas and beans, walks across the floor, and helps himself a second time. He has sympathy for the boy's fatigue. The ride from Juárez was long, the bus filled with noisy men in the aisles singing melancholy ballads with their guitars for tips. But the buses today are big and modern. The boy is used to the dilapidated ones they use in Zihua, buses with holes in the floorboards. Every window cracked and covered with masking tape. Smelling of raw chicken and sweat. The buses that run from the border have real sunshades, not a thin scrap of fabric or a piece of felt with stuffed bears pinned on for luck.

This boy is troubled. When the bus started up without him, the boy seemed almost relieved, a strange reaction it seems to Esquivel. He would have expected the boy would be anxious. He sits now, his eyes glazed with fatigue, but curious, listening. He is a young man, still on the fresh side of adventure, maybe his first woman waiting ahead. Esquivel would give much to be in the boy's place.

A curious movement halts him. Conchita has moved closer to a spot where she studies the faces of the men. There is a softening in her face tonight, a peace he has not seen before. Sometimes he fears for her. She seems so sharp and weary, so *unsimpatico* with the men and their lives. Of late, she has taken a stray pup into her room. He thought to disapprove, but something in her eyes warned him against speaking.

Juanita, too, seemed to defy his wishes, sneaking the pup bits of meat and bones when she thought he was not watching. If he did not know the two better, he might think that they conspired against him. But neither woman has great love for the other. Juanita does not willingly share her position with a *puta*. Conchita has youth in her favor. She is still graceful. Filled with an energy that makes him catch his breath.

But maybe he is wrong about the women. He remembers a day, a month earlier. He came downstairs later than usual, his belly roaring from bad meat. From outside the kitchen, he heard the sound of laughter and running water. On the back stoop, against the rising sun, the two women were sudsing their hair; Shampoo bubbles popped and slid over their bare shoulders.

He stood, paralyzed, trying not to breathe, the moment so perfect. For many days, he carried the vision of watching them laugh with no self-consciousness, with no idea of being watched. How long he stood there, he did not know. When they lifted vats of water onto each other, the water ran down their breasts, making hard puckers of their nipples. The line of Juanita's breast surprised him.

It had been a long time since he had seen her skin. He was used to thinking of her as an old woman, dried by the desert and her work, and he was surprised to see her skin, still fine and firm. Perhaps he had fallen into the habit of thinking of her as old because she has no children. He is not sure when the idea took hold, but there, in the soft light, her skin was as beautiful as Conchita's.

Juanita began to braid Conchita's long hair. When she looked up and saw him watching, she returned his glance without wavering, pulling the strands tighter and tighter until Conchita complained. He returned to the house to pour himself a cup of coffee, confused with the challenge in Juanita's look. The thought remained for many days— he had been staring with hunger at his own wife.

In the cantina, a sound intrudes. The men need attention. It is long after his closing hour, but the night seems ripe. Usually, he closes at the same hour each night, and the men pick up their drunken bones and return the way they entered, dissatisfied, melancholy, still searching for whatever they came for. But tonight, the cantina buzzes with energy that makes the thought of closing impossible.

Esquivel glances again at the boy. Perhaps he is considering his own story. The words seem close to the surface, but shyness defeats him. Whether he will speak is unclear. Esquivel makes up his mind to say nothing. A young man has the right to decide. A married man is always torn between the need to speak and the desire to say nothing, but the boy has no woman to confuse his nature.

Mendoza is like a cougar on the rocks as he begins a slow, lazy stretch. His legs are splayed out in front of him. He is aroused by the talk. It is like him to find only the hard sex in the men's stories. He slowly unsheathes his knife and pulls it in front of him so the firelight catches the edge. Without paying heed to the others, he brings the edge of the knife to the fleshy part of his forearm and scores a crosscut that lays open a crimson track. To prove his bravado, he lowers his mouth and sucks.

When he finishes, he swipes his mouth with the back of his hand, looks up to see Esquivel watching, and grins. "I drink my blood!" He belches hard and settles back, satisfied. It is on the tip of Esquivel's tongue to tell him to take his filth outside as Mendoza grins and waves his empty glass across the table. "You should be glad I don't pour my piss on it to heal. It is the *indio* way. Good for snakebites." He belches from his beer and settles back, satisfied that all eyes are on him. Esquivel brings a fresh *cerveza* and thinks he will kill him one day.

Mendoza has not noticed Conchita in the shadows. He brags that he can smell the scent of a woman from a long distance—twenty meters. Once, in a night of drunkenness, he sat at one end of the room, blindfolded, and won his next *cerveza* on a wager when Juanita innocently entered the far end of the room. Esquivel feels the same black rage as on that night. That a man should know such a thing about another man's wife fills him with disgust. Mendoza is an animal.

Mendoza notices the boy. "Hey, *perrito!* You don't talk much."

Taxco gives his lazy grin. It is easier.

"You want a turn with that woman upstairs? That why you here, amigo?"

Redness creeps into the boy's cheeks when the room turns its attention to him. His humiliation is tempered by pressure against his leg; the mongrel pup has wandered from upstairs and brushes against his side. He leans to scratch behind its ears, grateful.

Someone says, "Leave the boy alone. He don't hurt nobody."

Mendoza acts as though he doesn't hear. "Maybe you break in those *cojones* tonight, heh, boy? Give you something to take home for your visit? A souvenir?"

Jim intervenes. "Knock it off."

"You ever have a Mexican *puta*, boy?"

"Leave him be." The priest tries to settle it, but the matter is not closed for Mendoza.

"Keep your mouth shut, priest! This is a matter between men."

The priest observes Mendoza in the gloom. His words are soft and low, meant only for the one. "Maybe you carry the guilt for something you have done. Maybe this wears at your soul?"

"It's no business of yours, Priest. Keep your mouth shut!"

The priest will not be deterred. "God knows more than you think, Mendoza."

"Keep...your...mouth...shut!" This time, it is not anger that contorts Mendoza's face, but something else.

The others turn back to their drinks. Mendoza, too, but his hand trembles.

Taxco watches with curiosity, his fingers still rubbing the pup's ears.

CHAPTER NINETEEN

Cortesana: F. Coutesan, prostitute

Esquivel's offers no accommodations for the night. At the end of each day, the men must return to the door they left that morning. It is Esquivel's way. Conchita will serve a temporary need, but she is not the one to rely on when anger boils between a man and his woman. Not all of the men are married. Some have a woman, but they have not stood before a priest or judge. In refusing to do so, they proclaim their independence— proof they do not wear the face of domesticity. Sometimes, they tell stories of how their woman pesters them to marry in the church for the sake of children. Sometimes, though, the women do not care enough to take the insult of common law to heart.

Taxco dozes fitfully at his table. It will be another full day's ride before the bus he boards in the morning will take him to Zihuatanejo. The salt air of his village, mixed with the smoke from the slash-and-burn in the hills,

lodges on the back of his tongue. He has never considered it before, but tonight, he understands that to taste
one's birthplace is a sign of loneliness. He remembers
how it was each time he dove for the *langosto*, lobster. On
the table before him, a small dish of salt sits beside the
saucer of cut *limóns*. He presses his index finger into it.
The salt is coarse, full-bodied like the sea.

One memory recalls another. Walking along the
waterfront with no money in his pockets. The small fire
of burning sticks at the open *restaurantes* where thin strips
of beef seared on the adobe cooking plates. The aroma
wrenches his gut as he remembers. His mind visits the
plaza at midnight, and he hears the whistles of *la policía
turistica* as they direct the rush of cars and taxis after the
restaurants close. This is the best time of the day, when
the breeze picks up and the palm fronds rustle in the
darkness. In Zihuatanejo, he and his friends wait for this
time each night—when the women and their fretful
babies are gone, and the quiet dogs slip through the
streets.

In the cantina, silence lengthens. The potter, Lázaro,
turns to him and asks, "What of you, amigo? Maybe you
are waiting for a turn?" He is kind, implying that Taxco
has a story. No woman beats a path to Taxco's door. He
has no door for them to find. This fact bothers him more
than any other.

"I...uh..." The words stiffen in his throat. The cruel
one, Mendoza, sneers and shifts with impatience. But he
has not told his story either. Perhaps he plans some great
story to shame the others, but although he makes rude
noises, he does not offer. The handsome one, Lázaro, does
not press. He will accept Taxco's decision, whether to talk
or not. This makes it easier.

As Mendoza slumps against the wall beneath his
photograph of Pancho Villa, he reminds Taxco of the

zanates at Zihuatanejo, the black songbirds that strut along the beach, puffing their bodies to twice their size while the females watch. Before Mendoza, Taxco thought it was a good thing to puff up and fan for the females, like the lizards in the desert or the roosters in the backyards—a sign to the girls that he is sure of himself. But he sees Mendoza doing that and he knows he will find another way. Talking is not his way either—as it was not the way of the fishermen who returned to Zihua each sunrise with their catch.

He recalls watching them in the mornings, eating their *ceviche*, the raw fish chowder marinated in lime juice, drinking milk and playing cards, and laughing while their wives bartered their fish. The quiet ones let their wives do the selling. Maybe they did not talk because they had nothing to say. Like Mendoza.

Taxco considers whether he will tell his story. The men wait without expectation, and this makes it easier. He begins hesitantly. "I go home to be married next week." Once the words are out, they do not form such a lump in his throat.

The old *americano* extends his hand. "*Felicidades*." The priest looks pleased because he thinks Taxco will be married in the church. He smiles his encouragement. The others smile as well, all except Mendoza, who seems to have not heard. The men's reaction settles Taxco's mind. He will tell his story, and maybe some good will come of it.

"We were children together. Every day we swim. I show her how to climb the *coco* trees, to dive for the *langosto*, to catch roosterfish. She shows me how to weave the hammocks her aunt sells at the stalls. She was young, only ten. But she makes me want to do better. When I was sixteen, I travel north, to earn money." He pauses and tries to think of the words to use that will not expose his pain. Telling a story to strangers is difficult. He does not care to share all that is in his mind.

"For two years, I work, then I return to my village, Zihuatanejo. It seems as though I have been gone a long time. I notice the dirt roads and how the jungle burns heavy in the air. My bus, it takes seven hours from Acapulco. My friend, the girl I tell about, is still working in the stall with her aunt, but she has changed. Grown. Her—" He does not add that her father is not impressed with him. His daughter shows promise of beauty. There is a chance of a better marriage than to a slaughterhouse worker with the smell of death on his hands.

"For a year, I remain. But I do not make as much money as in the north. I return to the border, thinking it will be as easy as the last time. But this time, the *bordañeros* are better at playing the cat and mouse game. Twice, I am caught and sent back on a bus. The third time, I take my money and hire a *coyote*." He pauses while the blackness of his memory fades. He will not share that story.

"The slaughterhouse in Los Angeles has been fined for hiring men without permits. They do not help me to get a green card. One of my friends tells me it is easier if I go north to Paso Robles to pick the grapes. Or to Salinas to pick the lettuce. This is what I do. But I am angry all the time because I hate the work. I am born in a fishing town where the *cocos* and the fish are for the taking. Up north, I break my back, bringing food to the table of people who do not want me there. I come from a village where people know me. It is hard, living among strangers."

The priest nods. "I have been north. Zihuatanejo is better, I think."

"After a while, I start to have pride in what I do. It is a good thing, growing food. My boss likes me. I drive a tractor, and I am in charge of a crew, and the boss lets me drive his truck to town. He leaves me alone for most of the day"—he wiggles his flattened hand and grins—"*mas o menos*, more or less." The Americans smile as well.

"I send letters home to Elena and money to my mother. To make her life easier. And to show Elena's father I would be a good son-in-law. Apparently, I impress him better than I expect."

With the change in the boy's tone, Esquivel leans close. He is surprised the boy has said so much. He has much emotion hidden inside him. Esquivel understands this. He is the same, a listener. Perhaps that is what Juanita liked in him at first, that he was a strong, silent man. Maybe she thought of him as a blank tablet with no thoughts of his own. But when she discovered this was not true, she retreated, using silence to punish him for her disappointment. But he had not meant to betray her. He was only that, a quiet man.

"I get a letter from her father. I carry it in my pocket like a smoking cigarette until I think it will burn my shirt. And me inside. In the letter, he tells me he has found a husband for Elena. A man from Mexico City who owns apartments in our village. But he tells me her older sister will marry me and my family has agreed. He wants me to return to settle the thing."

He halts, and the room waits. Esquivel is ahead of the boy. He knows what comes next. He finds himself blinking rapidly, waiting.

Mendoza's voice is lethargic and flat. "A woman to cook your supper and to warm your bed." No one pays any attention until he adds, "One bitch-dog good as another."

"Shut up, you pervert," Lázaro growls.

Taxco Verones tenses and makes strong fists of his

hands, but he does not meet his tormentor's eyes. Neither does he show his thoughts.

When he sees he cannot get a rise, Mendoza gives a sharp laugh.

"I go to see Elena the last time I am home. We were in the house, her sister and the younger ones, the *niños*. Making tortillas. We sit at the table, laughing and talking while her sister rolls the maize out on *metate*. When it is time, Elena pats a tortilla as she has done many times. Her sister is faster, patting one after another, setting them on the clay plate over the wood fire. Making sure they don't burn. It is good, sitting there. Like I belong. Elena teasing her *hermano* with the flour she smears on his cheek. Then her sister chastises her in a sharp voice, a hard voice, looking at me as if to say, 'See what a child she is?'"

The boy studies his fingers, and when he speaks, his voice is barely heard. "A man can only eat so many tortillas. But I think without the laughter, I starve to death."

Mendoza's words, even under his breath, sound loud. "Depends on what else you ea—"

"Shut up, you sonofabitch!" In a single, lightning motion, the blonde cowboy splits the bottom of his empty beer bottle against the table. Gripping it like a shaft, he crouches and shifts his weight from one foot to the other. This time Mendoza is quick with his knife, slicing across the gringo's forearm with a light touch that merely hints at his ability, but enough to leave a bloodied track. The two glare at each other like matched roosters, sizing each other before the spurs are unsacked.

"Let it go, Mendoza." Esquivel hears his own voice, louder this time. His stomach roils with the recollection of a night when Mendoza caught a small desert rat outside of the cantina and brought it inside. He bit the head off and spat it onto the floor while the others laughed and prodded him on. Esquivel remembers that he did nothing. When he thinks of the occasion, it is as though he is watching himself watching Mendoza, and his anger is not just with the Mexican, but with himself as well.

"I said—let it go!" He repeats himself for the good it will do. But he makes a vow. Whatever the outcome of this night, Mendoza has drunk his last *pulque* at *Esquivel's*.

Mendoza does not take heed. "I'm going to kill you, pretty boy! Me and this *cuchilla*. We're going to cut out your tongue. See?"

"Go ahead—try. I can do some serious damage. Come on." Josh grabs the challenge like a small dog with a bone.

Esquivel cannot see why the blonde American can't leave the insult alone.

"You talk big for a woman, *perrito!*"

"You talk big for a pig's ass, Mendoza. Settle it."

Mendoza's harsh laugh slices the room. He throws his knife without removing his eyes from the cowboy's. It lands point first in the table, a weapon for whoever will have the courage to claim it. "Pick it up, you woman. Go for it. First one reaches it, makes the slice."

The cowboy glances around, and his eyes weigh the advisability of making a move in a room filled with witnesses. "You first."

Mendoza watches to see if this is a bluff. The two crouch, ready, neither wanting to trust the other. Finally, Mendoza's eyes narrow. "Not here." He shifts, a slight easing of his muscles, enough to show that he has made a decision. *Ojalá!* Soon. When the sun comes up, you die."

Tension infests the room. Josh shifts to slow the flow of blood on his arm. Esquivel hears the fear in his breath, but he does not move. The dark-haired American does not move either, but his friend coils like a rattlesnake. He will be the one to strike, foolishly, with only a broken bottle. If the cowboy moves, Mendoza will have more than blood on his knife.

Across the table, the young man gains courage from his drink, and his eyes flicker to Mendoza's chest, where strands of gold chain wink in the lamplight. Temptation tangs the air while he considers. Maybe he thinks killing a man would be no big thing. He is used to death—what is one more pig? The boy's eyes telegraph his intentions, and Esquivel shakes his head in warning. Mendoza would have his life before the boy could reach the spot where the knife stands.

Even drunk, Mendoza is not immune to the hatred surrounding him. He is tired, and he uses the pause as an excuse. When no one takes his challenge, he returns his knife to its sheath, and the men move back to their drinks. "This isn't finished, *perrito*."

A fog of tension clings to the men's faces and armpits until their fear passes and their labored breathing quiets. The rain torrents have ceased, but those still standing seem uncertain of whether to sit back down or to leave. The night is tired, as worn out as they are, but some are too languorous to find the door.

Esquivel frowns at the clock on the wall showing four a.m. The hour is late to send men into the darkness with so much liquor in their brains and no moon to light their path. The darkness hides the path of the water, and the sand will be treacherous, even when in daylight. He doubts they would leave now if he tried. Better to wait another half hour and send them off with a breakfast of Juanita's *huevos*.

In the meantime, he will find something to settle their minds. It is not good, the unfinished business between the little cowboy and Mendoza. He would not mourn the loss of either of them, but trouble will bring the authorities, and that will bring Juanita's wrath. He turns to the priest, who did not rise during the fight. The priest has spoken little this night, only to encourage and to sympathize. Maybe he, too, has a story of a woman. A long shot, but it is not inconceivable; priests have been known to stretch their vows to the limits of God's patience.

Esquivel has no sympathy with a man who willingly chooses celibacy. The word means to live unmarried; it does not mean to live without sex, but that is how the priests interpret it. Such men are fools. Better to shiver with the chill of an unwilling woman than to have nothing. Even though he is married to an unsympathetic woman, enough to drive any man mad, his memories sustain him. To think he could live a lifetime without even the memory of a woman's sex proves a man knows nothing of himself.

Esquivel expects from Juanita only the familiarity of her voice, a good meal, and the shared laughter of the past. It is good, working beside her each day, knowing she will throw off the covers, even on the coldest night, and start the stove if he needs a cup of hot water or a poultice, or a boil that needs lancing. A wife is comforting; a man who has none is to be pitied.

A man who chooses to live without such comforts—if there are such, they are saints. But this priest is no saint. Sitting in the gloom, he looks as much a sinner as any of the men—more than somen and *loco*, besides. The Mexican have a saying: *a man without a woman must scratch himself.*

Esquivel glances over to where Lázaro sits at a table, lost in the reflection of his memories. His story was animated, filled with smoothness of having been told many times before, but Lázaro's eyes have the look of a man who doesn't believe his own truth. Which of Lázaro's fancy women would lance his boils? With such women, it must be hard to keep up appearances. When he eats gassy foods, he cannot fart in his sleep. To have to watch every word, every moment—such a life would be difficult. Maybe the expression he sees in his friend's face is weariness. Maybe Lázaro is tired of always having the best.

"So what do you do?" Lázaro brings the boy back to his story.

"What do you mean?"

"About your girl, Elena? What do you do?"

"Maybe I go back and marry her anyway."

"She is willing?"

"Maybe. I think so. Yes." This time, the boy is certain. His Elena is not the kind to be swayed by a rich man with many houses. Her eyes told him this when she was ten, and she had not changed.

"Take her north," the one called Jim speaks.

Fire dies in Taxco's cheekbones, replaced by chalk. He thinks of his last crossing. The words grate in his throat. "No *coyote*."

"I can get her a green card." Jim again.

"How?"

"You good with cattle? I have a spot for a hard worker, wants to learn."

"In California?" California is a hard place to earn money with a wife. Easier to share a house with men, but he will not bring a wife into such a situation. His blood pumps hope. "I am a hard worker. Where in California?"

"Close enough to town. West of Fresno. I got a double-wide trailer. You're welcome to it. Rent included."

His friend Josh rises, anger in his accusation. "Thought you were going to rent out that place. Said I'd help out when you need an extra hand." He walks from the table to the fireplace, his lips pressed and angry.

Taxco studies his hands and tries to breathe. Shandon is west of Fresno. "I could do this. Like I say…am a hard worker. *Soy gallo*. I am also lucky."

"Good. I believe in fate. What's your name? Mine's Jim Patterson."

A *grillo*, a cricket, clicks in the corner near the fireplace. Before Esquivel can cross the room, the blonde cowboy crushes it beneath his boot.

Mendoza's anger fills the room. "Damn it, the cricket is good luck."

Esquivel has a mind to say the same, but Mendoza's rage consumes his words. He bends to toss the last of the wood into the fire and wishes he were somewhere else. Too late for the hunt tonight. Mendoza's dogs are safe for another day. He turns and sees Lázaro's unguarded expression; the potter is happy for the boy.

When Esquivel decided to marry Juanita, Lázaro was the one to say what the others were thinking. An Indian girl was no catch—he could do better. There were many times, later, when Esquivel might have agreed. But the early years were good—filled with more satisfaction than he sees in his friend tonight. Maybe it is only because the hour is late and Lázaro's stomach is empty, but his friend wears sadness. Each of his women is a steak, juicy, tender, and prime. Maybe for him, a steady diet of steak does not ease the longing for plain beans. Maybe in all his cooking pots, Lázaro does not find enough food. The thought makes Esquivel smile.

In the back of the cantina, his wife sleeps. She is a good woman. She cooks better than the others, and she asks for little. When she stays on her feet too many hours, sometimes her feet ache. In the early years, she liked it when he brought a basin of warm water and rubbed them with *manzanilla* soap. Somewhere—perhaps in the pile of rubble that needs to be burned—is an old porcelain pan. Perhaps when the sun comes up, he will find a minute to see what shape it is in. Maybe it has grown rusty after all the years. But maybe not. In the meantime, a room filled with edgy men who need their minds settled.

Esquivel pinches his thumb to his forefinger, a Mexican's warning that, shortly, something will change. "Padre, your turn."

CHAPTER TWENTY

Cortar: To gossip, to speak ill of someone

I n Casa Corte, no cathedral stands proudly against
the sky. Casa Corte has only a single church, a small
concrete building marked with a plain cross where
the Catholic faithful gather on Sundays at seven in the
morning—and in the summers at ten in the evenings as
well. In Casa Corte, the priest is required to do more than
perform the Sacraments. He must visit his parishioners'
homes when their tortillas are hot from the grill and the
noon meal is ready, not just when the babies are chris-
tened, or the ancient ones are dying in their beds.
Another church, a Jehovah's Witness Hall, lies sixteen
kilometers south. Most people line up on one side or the
other. Esquivel's cantina provides living faith for the rest.

The bar is silent for many minutes. The Mexicans idle
with their glasses while Esquivel waits to see if the priest
will begin. He has been enjoying Esquivel's *pulque* for
many hours and, even though drunkenness has a way of

pulling the secrets from the soul, an honest man, even a
priest, has no reason to fear. He justifies his visits to the
cantina by pretending to himself that he studies the ways
of men, so he is better able to save their souls. But, like
the men who hide their wedding rings in their pockets
before they visit Conchita, he takes off his collar before he
drinks.

"God help me, I listened as a man and not as a priest."
The priest keeps his eyes downcast as he repeats himself.
"God help me. It was as a man." When no one interrupts,
he continues from the corner table, where his face is
hidden by the shadows.

"It happened fourteen years ago. When I was twenty-
eight, newly ordained and filled with a zest for souls. I
had no doubt God meant for me to drive his lambs to
salvation. The indios I saw as fearful creatures. I as the
herder, pushing."

He pauses and stares into the fire, his face tense with
the effort of remembering. It is not an easy memory he
uncovers tonight. His thoughts are hard stones, set into
the brain for many seasons. Like the earth, the mind is
reluctant to relinquish them. Slowly, the flame works its
heat into his brain and his memories loosen. The muscles
in his face soften, and the years drop away.

"The bishop sent me to the area of San Vincenzo, a
pitiful area of little rain and less intellect. To learn humility, he told me. When my year ended, he summoned me
home to discover whether I had learned the lessons he
intended.

"I arrived at the bishop's house with only a handful of
possessions. My lack of worldly goods seemed to prove
that I had found his meaning. It was a logical mistake—I
thought so too. The bishop took from his cabinet a bottle
of fine brandy and poured each of us a glass. It was his
intention, he explained, to send me to a larger town, for

in his mind, I was destined for greater things. I secretly agreed, although I made no sign. The year spent among sheepherders and farmers had made me anxious. My ears burned with the fervor of sermons I had practiced on the peasants of San Vincenzo. Now my gift would be recognized."

The priest's face glows with the sheen of the firelight. His fingers absently tap his glass, but he does not drink.

"The morning of my first Mass, I looked out upon my curious flock and saw her sitting alone, slightly apart from the others, her face transfixed in prayer. I later learned her name—Señora Maria Estonia de Fernandez. It was fitting that she was named for the mother of Christ. In the early light, she appeared a manifestation of the Virgin herself. Her hair was covered by a white mantilla, but I could see her copper coils, heavy and shining under the beam of light from a nearby window. Speckles of dust danced in the air above her, like stars. It was as though God had halted the universe for that moment so I would understand the importance of our meeting."

Taxco listens with interest. Esquivel notices and wonders what value the boy finds in the padre's story. For him, one priest is the same as another, but the dust of the Casas Grandes plains has suffocated this one's pride. He seems little more than the burro he rides twenty kilometers to the Palanganas River to bathe, for pleasure, he says. The *americano* rises from his stool and hitches his hip, trying to ease the stiffness. He carries his glass to an empty table and slumps onto the bench with a sigh.

"Señora Maria...my Maria—for this is how I now regarded her. My Maria glowed with purpose and energy as she worked beside me, tending to the sick, seeing to the less fortunate, even feeding the pigeons in the courtyard. Each day, I strove to raise myself in her eyes, to prove my worth to her.

"In the weeks following, my fever grew. I warned my parish of grave sins hidden in their souls. I wagged my finger at those who misled themselves. The rotting of the falsely pious, I called it. I noticed with satisfaction that Señora Maria listened intently."

The priest speaks with the caution of someone used to drunkenness. Dissipation has sapped his energy.

"*Andale.*" Hurry up, someone says.

"Each Saturday, I heard confessions from three o'clock until evening shadows appeared on the cemetery wall. As each penitent left, I peered through the screen... hoping she would appear. I longed to hear her secrets. Shared with me and no one else—not even her husband. When she did not appear, I sought her out. When next I saw her, I chastised her in a mild manner. To stir her conscience.

"Finally, the day came when she appeared for her Sacrament of Penance. The luminary candles cast a glow on her face, and my heart leaped. Such was her voice. I closed my eyes and tried to perform the Sacrament. But God help me, I did not listen as a priest.

"I cannot tell you what she revealed. It is enough to know that she left gratified, uplifted. The next Saturday, she returned. Each time, I warned her that absolution required she confess every detail of her life. She was unable to bear children. A yearning that consumed her. All the village knew of this. I suggested the sin might be her husband's. My intent was to divide them so she would come to rely on me in all matters.

"I began to prescribe longer and longer penance. Whole strings of rosaries so she would be praying yet when the last person left. It happened as I hoped. Each time, I heard her voice softly reciting her prayers. Afterward, we would speak quietly, stolen moments that became my reason for being.

"When my sleep was restless and broken, her image would visit like the Virgin's. I began retiring earlier and earlier to my cell.

"We spoke often in passing. On the street, she accompanied by her maid. Or in the company of others at fiestas and social gatherings. Sometimes, I would take a word with her husband. Although my assistant, Father Riuz, thought him a man of honor, it took only a few discussions before I recognized the husband to be without faith. My vanity made this easy. I was intellectually superior to Señor Manuel Estonio de Fernandez, for all his wealth and aristocracy. After all—had I not attended seminary in Mexico City? And later spent a summer at the Basilica in Rome? I vowed to open Señora Maria's eyes to her husband's failings in order that she might protect herself."

A moth flutters from the chandelier and lands on Mendoza's shirt. He cups it clumsily and carries it across the room. Esquivel waits, thinking he means to toss it onto the embers. Instead, without speaking, he stumbles to the door and drops the moth into the darkness.

The priest continues as though he hasn't noticed the interruption.

"Each week, her small face would pale—her eyes would widen with fear as she considered my words. She watched me with such intensity, never moving. It was as though God sent her that I might realize my genius. Through Advent and into Pentecost, my admonitions gave way to stern warnings, and finally to ranting about the blackness of sin. Such power God had given me. I was determined to use it all.

"She began seeking me out, asking council on slight matters of conscience. Had she spoken of these in the confessional, I would not repeat them here. But she would watch for me in the corridor, pretending for the sake of those watching that she was merely spreading grain for the pigeons. 'Was it a sin to close a door in haste, to prevent the hens from entering her house?' Was this burst of emotion the 'rotting piety' that I warned against? 'Was the slamming of a door sin enough to prevent her from taking Communion in good conscience?' I encouraged her to seek me out each time such a thing occurred, and I would give absolution.

"She began attending Mass each morning, her eyes burning as though with fever. In my conceit, I thought she held a regard for me she could not conceal. Her skin became pale from long hours spent praying. Her delicate hands toiled ceaselessly, rubbing the statues of the saints with lambswool when we cleaned the church on Saturdays. Such days were bliss, the two of us working silently. Only the flickering of the candles for a *dueña*."

In the firelight, the priest's eyes recall the bliss.

"One day, she came to me distressed beyond reason." The priest's voice hardens. His glass trembles in his hand.

"Her husband had declared her faith obsessive. I was beside myself that an unbeliever would make such a judgment. She pleaded to know when her barrenness would end, and I assured her, 'In God's time.' She seemed unsatisfied, so I added, 'Perhaps God punishes the sins of your husband, not yourself.' Instead of calming her, my words seemed to distress her. I wondered what influence her husband was bringing to bear, and I questioned her about this.

"'He is not a bad man,' she said. 'He is a non-believer,' I insisted. 'Is it a sin not to practice Catholicism?' 'It is a sin to turn away from God,' I repeated. Infuriated that she would attempt to take her husband's side against God, I nearly shouted my response. 'Ask God why you have prayed so fervently and still no child fills your womb! Ask Him why your husband does not come to confess his sins and to do penance if he wants a child so badly.'

"Her face went ashen, and she collapsed, not into my arms where I could assist her, but against the pew. As if she preferred the coldness of the wood to my ministration. Tears formed a question in her eyes as she lay reposed in the wings of the angels. Never have I stood closer to the Blessed Madonna than at that moment. But it was not to last. As soon as her color returned, she gathered her skirts in her hands and fled down the aisle. Not caring that I called out for her to wait.

"The next time she appeared, I could see that things were not well in her household. The seed I planted had taken root. She confessed to me—not in the confessional, or I would never be able to reveal this to you—but as we each took an edge of the altar cloth to shake it. 'We are barely civil to each other. I find coldness in my heart that was not there before. Perhaps this is the sin of which you warn.' My response was soothing. 'Such is to be expected, my daughter. Your relationship is unevenly yoked. Does not the Bible warn of such?'

"She returned home to report my words to her husband. The following day, Señor Fernandez appeared at my doorstep, shouting vile warnings. The other priests managed to pull him off before he could do me harm.

"The next Sunday, I warned my parish that no one can serve two masters. To do so would jeopardize one's immortal soul. How Señora Maria blanched at my sternness. The color drained from her cheeks, and she lowered her head as she wept. Did I show mercy at her distress? No—I doubled my efforts, my voice thundering from the windows, frightening the swallows roosting in the rafters. So great was my pride. In my mind, I rivaled the Apostle Paul.

"Weeping, she leaped to her feet and rushed away before she could partake of Holy Communion. How distressed I was that she would forsake her Lord's sacred Body and Blood in this manner. After Mass, I made a visit to her house, intending to seek her confession. Instead, her husband came to the door. '*Vamanós*,' he shouted before I could explain. 'Get out and leave us. My wife was a happy woman before you came. Now she is a pitiful, moaning creature who thinks God is punishing her for living.' That he could describe my Maria in such a manner was proof of his blasphemy. But the husband was not finished. 'You will cease contact with my wife, or I will report you to the bishop as a womanizer and a defiler of virtue.' Only that, and he slammed the door.

"I was filled with indignation. Such blasphemy. His anger only reinforced my resolve. When next I saw Señora Maria on the street, carefully choosing *limóns* and beefsteak for her table, I attempted to have a word. 'No... I must not. My husband...' she told me, while her eyes betrayed her deep fear. I would have none of it. 'Come with me to the tabernacle. In the presence of God, you will know that my words are in your best interest,' I pleaded in the Lord's name. 'No...I cannot.' She stood, not meeting my eyes, her breast heaving. How I longed to take her hands and comfort her, for I could see what fear and loathing her husband inspired, how she was torn in her desire to be with me. The sanctity of marriage against the salvation of her immortal soul—such a dilemma even Moses could not have endured.

"From out of the crowd, her husband appeared,

kicking at the hens and roosters in the courtyard. Without ceremony, he grabbed her arm and half-dragged her, weeping, in the direction of her home. I made as though to follow, but Father Ruiz restrained me with a firm hand on my shoulder. 'Enough!' he bellowed. I was hard-pressed to understand his meaning. Was it not her husband who had transgressed the Almighty's commandment? Whatever abomination her husband intended for her, I could scarcely imagine. Yet here was my brother in Christ telling me to make no interference.

"I returned to my cell and paced while shadows filled the small window. I tried to pray, but instead, I found myself thinking of her translucent skin, her beautiful eyes, wide and filled with compassion. I demanded answers from God, insisting He free her from her yoke so we might work together for His glory. But even as I prayed, I knew what I wanted. And I knew, too, what the answer would be.

"After a fretful night spent tossing in my bed, I was awakened by a rap at the door. Delito, a small boy whom I was teaching altar service, stood before me, nearly hidden by a box tied with plain twine. What gift, this? I wondered. It was no occasion for gifts. Certainly not before I said morning prayers and made my ablutions. I resolved to set it aside and warned the child not to be late for Mass.

"He had no sooner departed before I turned to the box. A feeling of foreboding stealing my anticipation. I recognized my dear Maria's neat handwriting on the attached note. With trembling fingers, I pulled the string. When the twine fell to the bed, I slipped the lid from its place and set it aside. Hurrying to unbind the cloth. Inside—oh my god, such a travesty. Her hair, crudely chopped with a knife, or even a machete. Her lovely tresses, waist-length, scented with *limón* and rainwater.

"I was seized with a terrible rage so I could scarcely lift my hand. The weight was unimaginable. A woman's glory severed and desecrated! What sort of man would do this? That the husband's soul was irretrievably lost was a small consolation. Such a punishment would destroy her, render her a recluse, which was surely what he had intended. She would slowly decline behind her doors, ashamed to be seen! I imagined the tale the husband would spread about me, the speculation about our relationship when nothing impure had ever occurred. That he could have afflicted his rage on such a gentle woman! Revenge overtook my good senses.

"In a moment's time, I seized up my eating utensil, a meat knife of finest steel, determined to act as her avenger. Surely God would forgive me. As I gathered myself for this deed, I noticed the note, forgotten in my haste. I unfolded the paper and stared in disbelief."

The priest halts and stares unseeing at the table. Mendoza sneers at the room, but he gives up his chance. This tells Esquivel that he, too, is affected.

"Sometimes at night, I feel the tears—like hot irons. Sweet Jesus, the pain as I read. 'Dear Father Alberto, it is with humility that I come to understanding. My vanity has been great in thinking I was free of the rotting piety you warned of. For my penance, I will become a recluse, praying for the salvation of souls. Please pray for me. I have searched my heart a thousand times and cannot discover that of which I must repent. I will commit the remainder of my life in searching for that black stain. You are too good, too holy, to understand the deep regard in which I hold you. Jesus, Mary, and Joseph. In faith, Señora Maria Estonio de Fernandez.'"

"For two days, I remained in my room, suffering no one. No meal touched my lips, not even the tepid, stale water from my basin. On the evening of the third day,

Father Ruiz rapped on my door with great urgency to warn that Señora Maria's husband was searching to kill me. In order to forestall such a sin, I allowed myself to be bundled into an ox cart and to be hauled through the town like so much cattle fodder."

CHAPTER TWENTY-ONE

Corteza: F. Bark, crust, peel

The room waits, no man willing to break the spell that imprisons the priest. When the padre begins again, it is for himself.

"And that is how I ended up here, my friends, drinking in the shadows, seeking out the company of common sinners like myself. You speak of your woman, the lady who poured her love into you as though you were a holy chalice. I am here to confess I destroyed mine."

The priest disappears into the comfort of his inebriation. It is a place Esquivel knows well, having seen the priest make the passage night after night. Sometimes, he wonders if God will punish him for selling the poison that traps the priest's soul. He tries to see his alcohol as no different from the corn and rice that is sold at the market. Each feeds the body, only in different ways. If the priest were to overeat, he would become fat, the same with the *mezcal*. Who would think to condemn the seller of corn?

But Esquivel is not sure the argument will convince God.

The priest from San Lázaro slumps onto the table, engulfed by drunkenness. Esquivel knows the priest's story, the part he has not told—how he boarded the train at Chihuahua, west to Los Mochis through the Copper Canyon, peering out the windows at the Tarahumara who gathered. When it stopped for the night, he found a place to sleep beside the Indians camping near the siding. When they returned home the next day, he followed them to their canyons.

The priest jerks awake, roused by the stench of sweat, cigarettes, and the sound of Mendoza arguing over the drinks he has yet to pay for. The noise subsides, and for a moment, the only sound comes from the crackling logs. In his intoxication, he has confided more than he can bear. He keeps his eyes downcast and hopes the men will forget, but it is unlikely. A long-ago habit, he reaches into his stained trousers, into the pocket where he carries his rosary, but the pocket is empty. He has left his prayer beads on his bedside table.

Esquivel scans the gringos' empty bottles and the money scattered in front of them. They have not finished. A poor man keeps his *pesos* hidden, ashamed to have his *compadres* know how little he has. The proud man tosses his coin onto the table as though his pockets are bottomless. A cantina owner knows how to read the signs. When their glasses are empty, the gringos will welcome another round. He resists the urge to cheat them. When he hands back their change, he carefully converts their twenty-dollar bill into *pesos*. They are rich, but not so rich they haven't learned to work with their hands. He has seen their calluses, as rough as his and

Lázaro's in the field days. The gringos earn their money. He honors this.

He remembers the days when he worked in Mexico City, serving as a waiter in the home of Señor Madera, a family so wealthy that nothing was required of them but to hide their possessions from thieves. Señor Madera managed his wealth in clever ways. He hired people skilled in the methods of management while he smoked his Cuban cigars and encouraged his orchids and tropical fish.

To Esquivel, it seems the rich have only their money and their idleness to prove themselves. The thing that sets them apart is the luxury that allows them to do nothing. For a poor man to travel in such company, he must produce something of value. Perhaps he is skilled in conversation, plays chess, reads tarot cards in such a way that amuses, or perhaps he is needed to pour the drinks or carry the food to the table. But always it is necessary, this requirement to be useful.

The rich do not respect any work except to be clever, to grow richer, and to spend the hours drinking and amusing themselves. Something to occupy their minds. But they are jealous of their privilege, and they will set a servant out on the street to give the appearance of acting in the same manner. A poor man's legacy is the work he does, a rich man's, only his cleverness.

Mendoza leans back and laughs. "So, you come to the church of Saint Esquivel seeking absolution, do you, padre? I have news for you. There is no God. There is no one to hear your pathetic confession. You are doomed, priest. When you die, your soul will rot in some stinking black hole along with your hairless woman's."

The priest's face is florid.

"You are right about her. No one will want her now. Poor, stupid priest! Carrying your girlfriend's hair. I'll bet you still have it—in some stinking box hidden under your bed."

Mendoza is studying the priest the way he followed the moth before swiping it into his hand and setting it free. But he is not as kind to the priest. "You make an altar with it, don't you, priest? The closest you've ever been to a woman, and you can't let it go. Never spread yourself between the legs of a woman, huh, priest. Better go home and take your pleasure on her holy hair!" He laughs again, louder.

The priest slumps, too ashamed to face his tormentor.

Taxco Verones looks as though he will speak, but he remains silent. Esquivel knows the fear that cloaks the boy's indecision. The boy will be angry with himself tomorrow, like the disciples who denied Jesus at the garden. He will curse himself for his weakness.

The priest slumps against the wall, fighting the desire to turn on Mendoza and damn his soul for eternity. Anger tightens the lines of his face, thinning his lips and drawing in his cheeks. His tongue moves back and forth against the roof of his mouth. But he does nothing. Fourteen years ago, he seized his eating knife to avenge a woman, but tonight, he fights his nature.

No one speaks. It is just as well. The priest would not accept kindness, even if it were offered.

CHAPTER TWENTY-TWO

Corte: M. Court of justice

There is no courthouse in Casa Corte. Justice is meted out in the hope that a man's secrets will be kept. There is no such place where a man can be judged by his peers, only *Esquivel's*, where firelight casts truth in the shadows, and the prudent man heeds the covenant of the night. In the fresh light of day, a man knows his neighbor's sins, even as he maintains the illusion that he hides his own. In the hours before dawn, the night draws secrets from the soul, tempers discretion, softens the tongue. It is a man's way.

The men seem resigned. There is nothing to be solved in the hours that remain.

Lázaro speaks to his glass. "A woman likes a man to read to her. Especially poetry."

From a bench, the cowboy Josh rouses. He had not heard Mendoza's outburst. For him, there has been no interruption. "Had a woman, once. Used to write to me twice, three times a week. I was shoeing horses for the Feds, rounding up mustangs to be adopted out. It was a nothin' job, but I worked my ass off.

"She wanted me to write back, but mostly I didn't. She was a water tap, spilling words." He swatted at a moth and continued. "She quit after a while. Said she needed a commitment." He laughed, a hollow, mean sound. "I mean, I told her more than once I liked her. Figured if my feelings changed, I'd let her know."

Some of the men study their hands. They know the tangle in trying to satisfy a woman. Too often the words come back in a rush of anger or misunderstanding— things they said in passing remembered as promises.

Esquivel speaks his thoughts aloud. "It is hard to know a woman. She does what she wants."

The men nod. Better to leave the words left unsaid. A man will show his nature by his actions. A woman can see for herself the kind of person he is.

"Women...they like the details." Esquivel is not alone with his opinion. "A woman is about the small things." The others nod. "A new dress she wears for her man. It is for herself. A woman's nature flows from inside out. But with us, never. I want my guts seized with my first look."

Esquivel is silent. Lázaro is a hypocrite with his talk of clay and waiting. He is like every other man. A thousand things will catch a man's eye. He may smile and talk as though one has nothing to do with the other, but his eyes and his mind will stalk the woman like a hunter. He has watched the way a woman's lips part, the way she smiles, the way her breast heaves in response to Lázaro's voice. His friend's insides probably churn, but he waits. And the game is the best part a woman can offer.

"Passion is a young man's liquor. When our bodies grow old..." the *americano* raises his glass, "we turn to this." He sips his pain. "Love is different...it comes as easy at eighty as twenty. But the idea grows better with time. If I had only one pass at it..." He lifts his head and toasts his glass to Conchita. "I would take it now." The words seem heavy as they fall from the air.

The little cowboy is drunk, but his words are thoughtful. "A woman who gives up the game too fast spoils it for the hunter."

Mendoza surprises them when he agrees. "The hunter wants to take his time. Try out each of his weapons. The sex will be better if the hunt is hard."

The cowboy Josh is languorous; he doesn't appear to hear Mendoza. "Surprise...this is what a man likes in his hunt. A woman who surprises him makes the hunt one to remember."

His words bring the *americano* from his glass. "Most times, you come back empty-handed."

The cowboy considers his answer. "But there is always the possibility."

"Maybe I get tired, hunting for game I don't find," the *americano* says.

"Then you are not a hunter. You buy your meat from the market already cut." Josh toasts the air with his bottle, pleased with his logic.

"Maybe. Who's to say?" The *americano* crushes his last cigarette. "A man has to eat."

Mendoza's lips twist. Like a man betting, he tosses his last peso into the pile and watches to see where the cards fall. "To stalk a woman. To watch her eyes and know she has lost everything—even her hope. There is nothing else for a man." He smashes the table with his fist, pounding with each word until he pushes away and staggers to his feet, not pausing when the table crashes onto its side. When he manages to stand, he makes a move toward the little cowboy, and his rage ignites. "But you, amigo...you no hunt for the women. You are a *puta cabrón.*" This time, his words are not an idle challenge.

The little cowboy staggers to his feet while hatred spews from his black pupils. "What you call me, asshole?" Against his will, Esquivel backs away. Even the dark-haired cowboy does not interfere.

Mendoza welcomes the chance to kill—or maybe to die. The time has come. His laughter spills forth, and the overhead light catches a flash of gold in his open mouth. The cowboy gives a head-butt, and his forehead crashes onto Mendoza's face with a muffled crunch. A moment later, Mendoza spits two of his teeth onto the floor. He wipes a smear of blood across his cheek and swears. "You heard me. You are a *puta cabrón!* A faggot. You watch your friend like a man who keeps his kill from the buzzards. Does he know what he is to you, *puta?* That he sleeps in your head every night? When he mounts his woman, and you no exist?"

The stunned look the dark-haired cowboy gives his friend fuels Mendoza's laughter. He is right. The amigo did not know.

The little gringo reaches for his knife and slashes the air, opening a gash on Mendoza's cheek that splays blood onto the nearest table. In slow motion the two circle and parry, howling like two coyotes caught in the same box trap. Mendoza's gash opens, and he twists his head, trying to clear his vision. He backs up against the wall, trips over an overturned bench, and catches himself with a heavy elbow on the table, a clumsy motion that conveys his weariness.

The cowboy has the advantage. Twenty years and fifty pounds less flesh, and the blood lust of a man who has been pushed too far.

Esquivel feels his rage. A memory fills him, one he has been unable to shake in the hours that Mendoza has fouled his table. It is the look that Juanita gave Mendoza earlier, the rapid way she reacted—the movement of fear. He saw revenge in her eye. The memory sends a chill through his spine.

The cowboy pursues his advantage to the wall. When Mendoza can retreat no further, he slashes the air with slow, clumsy swipes until his arm is weary and the cowboy knocks the knife to the floor. He leans against the wall, all that supports him, and his oily hair shines in the light. His eyes, hooded by his scowl, do not meet his tormentor's.

The cowboy ignores his friend's pleading and presses his blade against Mendoza's jugular. His fingers twitch, but the knife fails to obey. For long seconds, he tries to push the blade to its conclusion, but even Mendoza's sneer cannot force the blade. No one moves. The death of Mendoza is the cowboy's decision.

"Let it alone!" Esquivel shouts, his words muffled as he snatches aside the newspapers under his counter. He rises, and the blood rushes back into his head. His fingers twitch, and the shotgun blast sends a muzzle flash through the barrel to the ceiling over Mendoza's head. In the silence, the spent shell hits the tile with a loud clink.

The cowboy releases his hold.

Mendoza turns. Esquivel feels his hatred coming alive. A patch of cement falls from the ceiling onto the floor where Mendoza is frozen. "I save the other shell for your cursed dogs!" No consequence too heavy for the exhilaration flooding his veins. "It is me who is looking for trouble this time!"

Mendoza blinks first, but it is not his fierce eyes that show surrender, but his trembling fingers. His growl is intended to draw attention from his own shame. When he fails, he uses his threats. They have worked in the past. "I'm going to kill you, amigo. Then I'm going to take your woman again."

This time it is not a tire iron in Esquivel's fingers, but the butt end of the shotgun. He raises it and tries to ram the wood against Mendoza's skull. In seconds, hands are pulling him off. He tries to wrench the barrel back, but many fingers pry it free. Other hands pull him backward, spin him around, and press his face against the cement wall. His friend Lázaro shouts a warning for him to be still.

Esquivel is surprised at his calmness. His muttered promise is for his ears alone. "Tonight, I go hunting."

The cowboy draws out his triumph. As he pulls the knife away, he wipes the blade against the front of the Mexican's filthy shirt, taunting him, drawing the blade down the exposed row of buttons, severing the thick cotton thread so they drop with a plink, plink, plink onto the tile. Mendoza, his head hung low, cannot help but hear the sound. The cowboy looks up at his friend and sees something in his eyes that releases his need to kill. Slowly, he rises to his feet, kicks Mendoza's knife under a table, and moves away. Mendoza slumps against his table. His head hits his folded arm, and he is still.

Esquivel watches closely. "He will not die inside my cantina. It would be a shame for the end to come so easily."

Josh tries to cup his friend's shoulder, but he is thrust off. "Come on, Jim. I know what you must be thinking. But look at him—the bastard's crazy." Josh's eyes convey his nervousness. It is for his friend that he spared Mendoza's life, a peace offering.

Jim cannot meet his friend's eyes. He rubs his palm against the leg of his pants and stares at the floor while his face flames. In the light of association, he is guilty. He should have seen the signs. But the cantina does not pass judgment. It is he who does that, on himself and his blonde friend.

No one speaks. Some of the men, like Lázaro, do not try to put themselves in the dark-haired American's place. Others, like the *indio*, can find no words.

For his part, Esquivel does not concern himself with the gringos. The dark-haired cowboy and his friend have ridden together from the border; they will have to settle their differences. If they do not, Chihuahua is a good place for a cowboy with a rodeo saddle to hitch a ride south. The people of Chihuahua are as honest as anywhere else. Someone will give the blonde cowboy a ride.

When he sees he can't break through his friend's anger, the blonde cowboy turns toward the door and slips into the pinking dawn without collecting his change from the table.

When he is gone, the men lower their heads and wait. It is good that Juanita is in the kitchen, rattling pans. The odor of *huevos* and *chili* wafts through the cracks of the kitchen door.

No words are spoken, but Esquivel understands. Even though he will tell his wife to carry a plate to the blonde cowboy, he gives him no concern. He does not care, one way or another, about the sexual inclinations of a man he does not know, but this one is not a man because he lacks purpose. Not every man is for making babies, but he needs to be useful. When the bull calves are castrated, they will provide food for the table. Juanita would say that a *puta cabrón* is an aberration against God. He is not so sure. This cowboy did not choose his passion; it has chosen him. But if he is not careful, the anger inside him will eat a hole in his gut, and he will be no good for anything.

Esquivel pushes a rag with the toe of his boot to wipe

the blood that stains his floor, then kicks it under Mendoza's table for the flies. It is not a good omen for The Day of the Dead. His wife will be upset if she sees, and he will have to listen. The idea makes him weary. He bends to pick the blonde cowboy's hat from the floor and hands it to his friend.

"What am I supposed to do with this?"

Esquivel shrugs.

CHAPTER TWENTY-THREE

Cortar: V. To die

There are no trees growing in Casa Corte, no forests to yield lodge-pole pine or cedar for building. No banyans or palms to shelter the houses, only the small, tortured pepper trees that bend to find shelter from the unforgiving sun. It is good to honor the harmony of the wood; a builder must make the effort. The energies, they are the same, those that breathe life into a tree and those that drive a man.

Under Pancho Villa's stern reproach, Mendoza stirs. His head is already swelling, one eye is swollen shut. He fumbles with the bloodied tatters of his shirt and tries to stand. "Hey, *Bastardo*! Tell the woman get some coffee ready. *Comprende*? I go take a crap. Then we see what that *puta* upstairs has ready to eat. Some hard eggs, for sure." He tosses his knife on the table. "Anybody tries her before me—you slit their throat! You hear me?" His laughter fills Esquivel's doorway.

On the other side of the room, Conchita presses herself against a wall, her face impassive. The *americano* cannot bring himself to look away from the outline of her legs beneath her sheer dress. He raises his drink and studies her through his trembling glass.

The priest watches Mendoza's exit with dull eyes. Perhaps he considers the idea of following him outside. It is his usual hour for waking. For Esquivel, as well. He and the priest have more in common than either would admit. Although it is hard to be the man that God intends them to be, it is easier in the hour of sunrise than any other time of the day. Daylight and life have a way of corrupting.

It was in the priest's eyes, that he quails for the day when he will stand beneath his God's censuring gaze. But if the priest's God was not merciful, He would long ago have dusted this one from the earth. The thought pursues Esquivel as he watches the priest stagger to his feet and find the front door.

The priest returns. One after the other, the *americano*, Lázaro, Taxco, and the dark-haired cowboy wander outside to catch the first rays of morning while they empty their bladders into the sand.

Esquivel grows impatient for them to leave. He listens for his wife in the kitchen, but there is only silence. He calls out, "Juanita? The men wait." Maybe their stomachs are too sour for food, but he needs the reassurance his wife's presence will bring. It is still dark, with only enough light to discern the shapes of the mesquite bushes on the other side of the yard. In a few minutes, each man will be driving east into the rising sun.

The cantina fills with the aroma of fresh roasted coffee percolating in the battered coffeepot Juanita sets on the countertop alongside a jug of thick cream. She moves about the room collecting dirty glasses, her expression impassive.

From the window, Esquivel notices a solitary cloud serving no purpose except as a reminder that the storm has passed. The sight encourages him. He is eager to walk to the arroyo and see what changes the floods brought during the night. As a young man, he climbed the steep walls of the arroyo and watched the flash flood ripping through the canyon. The monsoons that carve out the earth and wash away his neighbor's livestock are gone in a few weeks. By January each year, the canyons are silent again. There was a time when he would walk out into the desert at sunrise to watch the thunderheads fill the sky with their strong, angry warning, but today, he has no such need. The storms are still majestic, but he has become the solitary cloud.

His head feels heavy, his thoughts ramble. He hears sounds in the kitchen and knows the routine his wife will follow. The stove will heat the room. When the frijoles are steaming in their skillet, she will cast off her shawl and toss it on the back of her chair. By the time the sun streams through the window, if she is wearing her light skirt, the sunlight will warm her through the thin cotton. His head fills with the image of her legs, smelling of *manzanilla* soap and musk. The thought brings a smile, the first in many hours. Maybe he is a potter as well.

Something has changed with the sunrise. It is the time of the morning when he should be outside, waiting naked in the yard, but today he has no need. Perhaps no need tomorrow, either. He has changed as well. The desert gives a better sunrise than at Acapulco. The beach shows a beautiful sunset, but it is the desert that delivers the promise of each new day.

The men are back inside with full bellies, all except the blonde American, and he is better off outside. His friend will pay for his beer. Mendoza is not back, either. It would be like Mendoza to leave without paying for his last round. The debt will never be collected. Better that Mendoza left without eating the platter of *frijoles* and *huevos* that Juanita set at his table.

On her way back to the kitchen, Juanita laughs at something Lázaro has told her. The sound surprises Esquivel. It is the honest sound that a child makes, happiness without any reason. She sounds settled, at peace with herself. Perhaps she slept more soundly without him snoring beside her. He expected her to glance in from the kitchen before she started the coffee, but it seems she was not concerned. The thought occurs; maybe it makes no difference where he spends his hours. Maybe she prefers the bed to herself.

He checks himself in the mirror that hangs behind the bar, between the shelves he built with his own hands while she handed him nails. On that day, he tried to impress her with his skill so she would not lose interest and return to the kitchen. The memory of her admiration is still there, in the wood. After the varnish dried, he caught her stroking it with the tips of her fingers, her hair knotted with a piece of yellow scarf. Yellow is a good color for a brown woman.

Across the room, the fireplace is a flat pile of ashes. He debates whether to toss in another stick, but if he does, it will smolder. Better to trust the heat that sleeps in the ash. No matter how flat the fire grows, a spark slumbers, waiting for the puff of air that will fan it into flame again. The line between death and life lies in the absence of breath. He thinks about this as he picks up a puppet tangled in its strings. A cantina filled with men is no place for children's games. Juanita was *loca*. Last night, her angry jaw sent a message, and her eyes glinted in the darkness. Even Mendoza, lust spilled from his eyes, fouling the air, a coyote's way of hiding in the darkness.

Mendoza. The word turns him cold. He hears a crack in his hand. He has broken the puppet.

In the open doorway, a dozen flies hover, unwilling to trade their freedom for the smells of sweat and food inside. Esquivel moves toward the door. He feels stiffness in his joints like the old *toreadors'* bulls on the *estancias* to the east. At the tables, the men sip coffee. Bloodshot and haggard, they sit without speaking. Mendoza's folding knife is gone from the table.

Esquivel makes his way to the outhouse, his bladder pressing inside him like an overfilled *bota* bag. He pauses at the door, annoyed by the stench. Someone has soiled the toilet in their drunkenness, another job for Juanita. It is a wonder she does not complain more than she does.

He opens the door and stares for a moment before he shouts, *"Dónde está? Qué repugnante!* Look at the flies. It's Mendoza! Son of a bitch!" His shout brings the others.

Mendoza's knife lies inside, the gore of his innards cloyed on the blade. His throat has been slashed. Already, the flies lay their eggs in the blood. The man's chest may bear another stab wound; Esquivel does not move the torn shirt to see. The man is dead.

Esquivel stares at the body, but he can summon no more regret than if one of the dogs from the arroyo were lying at his feet. He glances away, and his fingers twitch. What was it Mendoza said—his wish to see the dawn? The image is almost real, Mendoza emptying his bowels into the Chihuahua sand without realizing the desert was ready to swallow him as well.

Against the outhouse wall, flies cluster on the drying blood.

Chapter Twenty-Four

Corte: Weeding out

E*l policía.* Carlos Fuentes arrives in a battered Chevrolet, its headlights lacquered with road grime. He climbs from the worn seat, hitches his gun belt, and walks fifty paces to where the men wait. His talk is casual, unconcerned, as though he finds a dead man in every outhouse he visits. "Trouble, eh, Esquivel? Not often at your place. Fitting today—the fiesta. Padre... this is a busy day for you. Let's take a look."

"It wasn't me. I swear...it wasn't me." The blonde American stares from the window of his friend's pickup. The dark-haired American has found him passed out in the seat. His words are slurred. Esquivel watches as Jim Patterson wipes a flick of blood off his pickup door and looks up to see who notices.

Esquivel studies the others. No one will make trouble. They will pass the death off easily. He speaks for all; "Mendoza brought it on himself."

Fuentes squints into the gloom. "Mendoza, eh. So the dog is dead. No great waste." He looks around at the seven men. "So, which of you takes credit for this sack of shit?"

No one moves. Fuentes pulls Mendoza's yellow scarf loose from where it is stuck to the blood. The victim's shirt falls open of its own accord; there are no buttons left to unfasten. He glances at the bruises on Mendoza's face, the blood matting his filthy hair. "Someone stabs with vengeance. Any of you got more reason than the other?"

No one moves. No one makes mention of the word *asesinato*, assasination. It is *muerte*, death, pure and simple. With Mendoza's death, the past hours were, in hindsight, a trial. The men understand the difference between death and execution. Justice has been served.

El policía is unhurried. He has nothing better to do this morning. Awakened by Juanita's phone call, he was ready to get up anyway. He will drink coffee with his friend Esquivel in a few minutes, and his head will become clearer. He speaks cautiously to the blonde cowboy, noticing that the others have shifted in his direction. "*El muerto* was stabbed here. See the tips of his boots? Clean. He was not dragged here. He is a heavy man. A small man could have dragged him. This your work, *gringo*?"

The cowboy Josh shakes his head, his face paler than the peaked look of a man who has slept for only an hour.

"That Mendoza's blood on your shirt?"

The blonde cowboy looks down at the blood on his arm. "No, sir!"

El policía is gratified by the "sir." He turns from the cowboy and studies the others. "Padre? You got any ideas?"

The priest slowly shakes his head. "That is for God to judge. Maybe we can lay him out on the sand. I need to perform last rites. Perhaps the soul has not yet left the body."

"Mendoza had no soul."

The stench catches Esquivel. Taxco seems less affected. He is used to the blood of pigs. They each take an arm and help lower the body to the sand. Juanita is waiting with a few drops of water for the priest. He blesses it and sprinkles Mendoza. In the sharp air, the water sits on the skin like dew.

Fuentes stalks from the cantina door to the outhouse, then back again. "Nobody saw nothing out here this morning?"

"No. Nothing."

He turns to the blonde cowboy again. "You were asleep? In your truck?" The cowboy nods. Fuentes walks to the door of the pickup, then back to where the men wait.

The cowboy Josh catches Esquivel's eye. When he speaks, his voice is pitched higher. "I didn't do it. I swear." He turns to his friend, Jim. "Hey, you know, buddy...I wouldn't kill no one."

His friend says nothing.

"Hey...no one blames you. He was a bastard. His wife won't care—his daughter. No one will." Lázaro says.

"I didn't kill him! One of you did it. One of you."

"Sure, amigo. Sure. We were all drunk. Could have been any one of us."

"You weren't drunk, eh, Esquivel?" Fuentes straightens and stares at Esquivel. Esquivel does not drink. Not since his wedding. Only to taste the *pulque* before he serves it to make sure it is ripe. "This is not the work of a drunk. It is the work of anger. Someone had reason to kill this one." He glances toward Juanita, and Esquivel feels a quiver travel down his spine. He moves toward his wife, but the lawman's attention does not linger on her.

"It would be a shame—one of our lives for Mendoza's!"

"Maybe. Maybe not. *A la buena de Dios.*" *El policía* is not prepared to say. Guilt is about not having a good reason. Maybe they all had one. God will judge, and He is not here today. In five minutes, everyone will scatter, some into the desert, some to their beds. Let God speak now if He feels the need; *el policía* has other duties to attend to. The truth is for a judge, if there is enough evidence to bother.

Another matter, more urgent, occurs as he considers his obligation. "Mendoza has the fighting cocks. Valuable birds. They will be out of water. A lot of money tied up in those things. Someone will take advantage of the situation. Maybe I better take custody before word gets out." His eyes sweep the group, but he finds no resistance. "Leave word with Esquivel here where you will be. *Comprende?*" He squints at the blonde cowboy and his friend, Jim Patterson. "*Cortarse.* You let me know where you are staying." They nod.

To Esquivel, he says, "Sometimes a man dies, and that's the end of it. Was another killing, thirty-five years ago, down in the jungle near Acapulco. I was new on the force then. We never solved that one, either." He glanced up. "We heard it was an American kid was involved."

The light is anxious this morning. Esquivel can feel its hesitancy as he waits for the sun to warm the chill that engulfs him. The river of water from the mountains has disappeared into the ground; the desert is resting from a hard birth. Later, when the men come to his cantina, he will laugh and tell jokes and exchange news, but for now, he is silent.

The priest says, "I will be in my confessional tonight at ten."

The priest will wait in the empty church for someone to confess, but they will not come. Maybe God will forgive the killing of Mendoza easier than He forgives the blonde American cowboy for being a *joto*—maybe. This is one of those times when Esquivel does not try to understand God.

Esquivel hears Lázaro Quezada agree to deliver the news to Mendoza's wife—and to the daughter with the crippled foot—and something clicks in his memory. When Lázaro is drunk, he talks about the crippled girl. Perhaps he has imagined his hands sluicing her, making the pot whole again. There is something about her that satisfies his artist's eye. Perhaps this is what has troubled his sleep so many times in the past months.

Jim Patterson stands with his hand on his pickup, but he doesn't meet his friend's eye. "I ought to head on. Don't see much point, things being what they are. I need to take a look at those bulls of Señor Castañado's, over in Gordo."

His friend Josh stands, legs spread, fingers in his pockets, his hat low on his forehead, shading his face. He straightens and tosses his cigarette into the sand, and for a moment, it continues to glow, then burns itself out while both men watch. His shrug seems unconcerned. "You go on then. Reckon I'll head on down to the rodeo and try my luck. Might be my last rodeo."

While the blonde cowboy pulls his saddle from the pickup bed, Esquivel takes a ragged scrap of blanket from his wife and covers Mendoza from the flies.

Jim Patterson watches Esquivel, then turns toward his pickup without looking at his friend. "I'd go with you, but I'm getting too old for this. Jenna's been after me to quit. You might have better luck without me."

His friend Josh raises an arm in acknowledgment but doesn't turn around as his boots churn patches of sand along the roadway.

The priest from San Lázaro looks haggard. Tonight is the fiesta, and he will need a nap before the festivities.

Esquivel walks him to his car. He opens his mouth to ask a question but closes it again. He won't ask about the rumor; it is only women's talk. Even if Juanita claimed to have heard from Mendoza's wife, herself, that it was she who crippled the daughter, tugging the child away from her angry husband. Either way, the guilt was Mendoza's. A man like him, like Ray, deserves to die.

He sees Juanita studying the blonde cowboy with such intensity that his suspicions are roused. He turns to study the river, something to occupy him so he will not have to answer the challenge he sees in her face. Near the highway, the little cowboy stands with his back to the cantina, his saddle slung on his shoulder, a valise in one hand. Juanita does not speak English with enough confidence to approach the boy, but she knows who has done this deed. She watches the boy while a dozen cars pass, until a pickup jerks to a stop, waits for him to climb in, and resumes its journey south toward Chihuahua. When she turns back, Esquivel does not meet her face. He knows her well. They will not speak of this again.

The *americano* is the last to leave. He emerges from the cantina, his face rested from the hour he has spent upstairs. Conchita walks beside him. She carries a sack with her belongings, which she holds against her dress, while the *americano* explains in English, "No hard feelings, but she says she's coming with me."

Esquivel feels his gut knot. To his right, Juanita straightens. She has left her hair loose this morning, has not yet taken the time to braid it. That he notices such a thing does not strike him as odd at this moment.

CHAPTER TWENTY-FIVE

Cortar: To harvest, to pick as fruit

Later, after the funeral parlor has taken Mendoza so the villagers will have a real body for the coming procession, Esquivel returns to the kitchen to eat the tortillas and beans his wife sets before him. She is a good cook, better than a hundred other women. He tastes the tortillas and thinks to tease her with a dab of maize on her cheek, but he loses his nerve. When she reaches close to refill his plate, he presses thick fingers against the small of her hand. Her fingers are short, rounded by work. The thought occurs to him that he should have named the cantina *"Juanita's,"* for the work she has done. But she would have objected.

He still holds her hand, and she has not moved away. Her face is relaxed, soft like when she sleeps. More thoughts fill his head. Once the celebration starts, and the fireworks, there will be no peace. If he is to take any rest, he will need to do it now, when the sun is only half inclined to begin its journey.

The stillness reminds Esquivel of the day he first noticed Juanita running alongside the bus from Acapulco, her brown legs lifting her huaraches as she covered the sandy miles, a crucifix on a chain bobbing against her small breasts with each step. An older boy ran beside her, his plain white shirt and trousers a stark contrast to the vivid scarlet, purple, and greens woven into her skirt. Rarámuri, in their language, the runners. The indigenous people of the Copper Canyon.

It would have been nothing for the bus driver to stop and open the door of his half-empty bus for two more, but he used his authority to deny them. She ran the remaining twelve kilometers with sweat beading her beautiful skin. Later, while he stood sweltering in the strange heat, she pumped cool water from the communal well and shyly offered him a drink.

Two years later, it was her brother, Tiacuache, who brought her to the fiesta in Creel to celebrate when he and another Tarahumara boy won a 100-mile race in Colorado, in their thick huaraches soled with the discards of recapped tires. Esquivel caught a ride with a carload of his friends. The winners were small and shy until they began drinking the local brew, *tesqüino*.

The town square smelled of fermented corn. The villagers had germinated the kernels in plain, tight-lidded baskets. In the dark, so the buds did not become green and the beverage bitter. After the corn boiled for eight hours, they added *madroña* seeds and grass to create a milky white liquor with the kick of an angry burro.

He recalls the prayer the holy man gave before the first drops were offered, words he had Juanita write on a piece of parchment paper after he taught her the letters. The prayer hangs framed on the wall of his cantina.

We have been seeded, we are not born by our own virtue.
Drink with calm, speak with calm, count with calm. Drink
tesgüino to put happiness in your hearts. Get well drunk,
but lie down and sleep. Return tomorrow to your homes.

The celebration party began with Juanita casting soft eyes at him while one of the men passed him a small jar of *tesgüino*. He sang, danced, and watched the winners of the race grow to manhood with the strength of the brew. To the best of his memory, he obeyed the prayer-man's advice.

The next morning, he woke alongside a dozen Tarahumara. The milky beer had tasted like horse piss going down. In the morning, he felt it sloshing in his sour stomach while he stumbled blindly through a maze of cobbled streets. The girl's brother led him to a trail at the edge of the clearing, the Urique Canyon. Despite a head that threatened to split open, Esquivel followed him down the steep trail, through pine and oak, to a small rock cabin where Juanita and her family waited with a meal of corn and beans, and more *tesgüino*. This time, he drank water.

Juanita was ready for a husband. Her attendance at the party was an announcement of sorts. Esquivel's hung-over brain grasped the significance, and he smiled wanly at her father.

She joined him and her two brothers for a ten-day hike along the Mesa de Arturo Canyon, where they descended into a steaming tropical forest. By the time they emerged, close to Cerocahui, his hamstrings were stretched, his body numb from humidity, and his stomach had shrunk with the small amount of corn they boiled each night to supplement their fish and berries. But there was no more *tesgüino*. Not until the wedding, the brothers explained. He had proved his mettle to the satisfaction of the family, and they to his. He understood without words. *In the canyons, the Tarahumara prevail.*

When he could walk no farther, they stopped beside a thermal spring, and he threw himself in, clothes and all, and allowed the warmth to restore his aching muscles. How long he lay there, half-asleep, soaking heat into his pores, he did not know, until a sound woke him. Juanita waited, naked and honey-skinned, her quiet eyes shining with a mixture of eagerness and uncertainty. Her small breasts were peaked and anxious, her hair loosened, the ends teased by the waterfall's spray. Her small legs met at the apex of soft shadows. She reached for him, and he realized she was no longer a child, but a woman whose mystery had flowered. The brothers were elsewhere; he knew this by her eyes.

After their marriage, six babies grew inside her, but each failed suddenly in bloody flux, usually in the night. The doctor thought because she was a runner, her tight muscles interfered. Juanita would not accept a Mexican doctor's opinion; she sought out the healers in her village. "The house is so big," she fretted one morning as she faced the stairway to the second floor, where she rarely went except to dust. "Life grows best in small places," she whispered.

"The house is not responsible." Her ingratitude angered him. There were a hundred women who would favor such a house. "You need to eat. You are young enough—maybe you grow taller, your body can feed a baby."

Her coldness began when she reached the age where babies seemed unlikely. When winter passed, and the summer sun burned the geraniums outside her window, the chill had already taken residence. At first, Esquivel made pains to keep himself presentable in case she rolled to meet him. He showered and combed his hair every night, but the weeks turned to months without her touch. Each time he reached for her, it was for a simple need, soon satisfied. He found little satisfaction in the deed until, finally, it was no longer worth the effort.

The thing about the desert is that the seasons come and go.

He hesitates, aware of his grime. Juanita gestures to the water heating on the stove. A bath would be welcome. She finds a bar of palm oil soap while he undresses and climbs into the bathtub. While his mind drifts, he feels the pattern of her hand, circling, massaging until his skin is drugged. The soft kitchen sounds are for the two of them only. Conchita is gone. Soft and knowing, Juanita directs her fingers to the spots where he is sorest. At first, it seemed strange that she would know, but who better? She is his wife—his woman.

THE NIGHT HAS HELD off as long as it can. Now the sun has crossed to the far place beyond the ridge. Sounds of children fill the air. The sound of drumming and *mariachi* strings crawls toward the cantina. Esquivel stands at the door and studies the street where his wife's geraniums hold the night air in their stems. He feels the sap flowing through his own stalk, feeding his lungs and his limbs, feeding his manhood. The children's laughter draws closer and mothers admonish their young to behave. Fathers, for the most part, wait at the cemetery gate for their families. For the most part, the men do not take part in the procession, but later, they will teach their children to light off the fireworks. They will drink *cerveza* in the company of their dead parents and grandparents, toasting to the spirit of memory.

The parade advances, and Esquivel feels his anticipation. He has never felt the need for the crowd, but tonight, their happiness crackles in the air. Sulfur catches in his nose like the smell of gunpowder, and he wants to join the battle. Paper *maché* skeletons dangle from sticks. A proud-eyed boy dances ahead of the others, his skeleton bearing the bloodied scarf of Mendoza. The noise grows into clamor, more than he can bear. "Juanita...come!"

Juanita eases through the door behind and joins him. She wears one of Conchita's hair ornaments behind her ear, a paper hibiscus blossom left behind. It is pinned to her unbound hair, giving her the glow of a girl. She has changed into her Sunday skirt, and her blouse is loose and resting on her shoulders. He slips his arm around and pulls her to his side. In a moment, they are among the shouting, waving revelers. He tries to recall the hymn the others sing, but the words are lost to time. Juanita's voice carries above the others.

Ahead, the casket of Mendoza is borne by six teenagers. Señora Mendoza and her daughter follow, their expressions hidden in the mantillas that shroud their hair and faces. Lázaro Quezado walks beside them, his face shining with satisfaction. Esquivel starts toward him until he feels the tug of his wife's hand on his arm. She shakes her head. *No. Leave them to make their own way.* She is right. Tonight, he has enough for himself.

A village child hands him a small candy with his name written across the skull. One of his neighbors has included him in their family's festivities. When the child turns to Juanita, Esquivel folds his fingers around the candy. Not for eating, this one. He will place it behind the bar as a remembrance.

The procession makes a straggling turn toward the cemetery, where the men wait with supper baskets and fireworks. Already, they have begun lighting off sparklers. A man, already drunk, launches against him and straightens. It is Tonió Orosco, the wood hauler's grandson. Esquivel salutes him, and together, they watch as Mendoza's casket is lowered into the ground. It is a night for remembering.

Life is made up of brief moments, any one of which might appear to be a random matter, one moment followed by another with the effect of altering life. Today has been one such day. The air is acrid with the smell of gunpowder, the same as in the time of Pancho Villa. Laughter and drunken shouts charge the air with the energy of life and hope. In the darkness, Lázaro pulls Mendoza's daughter into his embrace and points out a blazing firecracker in the distance. The girl nods shyly, and the mantilla slips from her shoulder, her grieving forgotten.

The air is anxious this evening, like a virgin before her first kiss. Esquivel feels the mood and pulls Juanita closer. Something he once read occurs to him, and he leans to share his thought with his wife, who will not understand the meaning but will appreciate the gesture. *Always there is the new day. Whatever else the night brings, it surrenders to the dawn a fresh beginning.*

A Look At: Norske Fields
A Novel of Southern California's
Norwegian Colony

Discover the captivating journey of Norwegian immigrants forging their legacy in the land of bright horizons and unforgiving earth.

In 1888, five determined bachelors embark on an epic adventure, leaving Stranda, Norway, to fulfill their dream of becoming American land barons. Pooling their resources, they make an affordable land purchase in southern California, relying on a draw-from-a-hat method to determine who will tend to the superior land and who will make do with the less favorable plot.

Soon after, their sweethearts join them from the homeland, and the Norwegian Colony is born.

Written by the great-granddaughter of Nils Olsen and Ellen Fjorstad and a 2021 Will Rogers Medallion Award finalist for Inspirational Fiction, *Norske Fields* uses modern fiction techniques to recreate unforgettable characters who experience heartbreak—and bask in triumph.

AVAILABLE NOW

ABOUT THE AUTHOR

A fifth-generation Californian, Anne Schroeder's love of the West was fueled by stories of bandits and hangings, her great-grandfather and his neighbors working together to blast the Norwegian Grade in Southern California out of solid rock, Indian caves, and women who made their own way. She worked her way through Cal Poly University with a variety of odd jobs that included waitressing at a truck stop cafe in Cholame—near the spot where James Dean died.

She recently served as President of Women Writing the West, and her short stories and essays have appeared in print and online magazines. She has also been awarded several Will Rogers Medallion Awards and LAURA Short Fiction Literary Awards for western and inspirational fiction.

Anne lives in Southern Oregon with her husband, dogs, and free-range chickens where she volunteers regularly for the St. Vincent de Paul soup kitchen.